CHARMS & CHAPTERS

ALEXANDRA RUSCH

ISBN: 979-8-218-78220-7

For Nikki

CHAPTER 1

DANI

When the bell on the door to Charms & Chapters Bookshop tinkled, Molly let out an excited bark and her feathery tail started thumping the edge of her dog bed. I put down the stack of books I was shelving and walked around the corner to greet the only person who would get that reaction, my soon-to-be stepmother, Sara Maloney.

"You guys are back! I can't wait to hear all about your trip!" I exclaimed and grabbed her in a bear hug. "We both missed you so much. We meaning Molly and me." Molly was Sara's six-year-old golden retriever, and I'd been dog sitting while my dad and Sara went on a book tour. My dad, Erik Hanson, is an author and just released the book he wrote while we lived at our beach house in Lavallette, where we met Sara.

Sara hugged me back as tightly as I held her. "I am so glad to be back, and I missed you too! And yes, Molly, I get just as sad without you."

She scratched Molly behind her ears, a favorite spot, and Molly let out a small moan of pleasure. "Ready to go home, girl? Dani, let me bring her home and get her settled. I'll be back shortly and tell you all about the trip, okay?"

I shooed Sara out the door after she clipped Molly's leash. "Go. I'm putting some new books on the shelves and then I was going to make a pot of coffee."

I knew the promise of fresh coffee would lure Sara back to our bookshop quickly. She loves coffee almost as much as she loves my dad. And me. And Molly. Of course, I can't forget our bulldog, Tank. Ours is a blended family. Sara owned Molly and my dad owned Tank when they first met.

My mind wandered back to the summer Sara entered our lives and made everything better. I didn't know where I'd be now if magic hadn't happened on that slender strip of Jersey shore. But I knew my dad had never been happier, and even though I already loved Sara a lot, just seeing him enjoying life made me love her even more.

It hasn't always been a smooth path. In the aftermath of the hurricane that finally united us as a family, we drifted between our two homes next door to each other, Sara unable to break her rental lease on the Pendleton and my dad in the middle of rehabbing his, plus writing his latest book. In September, Sara officially moved into my dad's house, and I tease her all the time that they're living in sin. I won't be able to do that much longer, though. Their wedding is less than a month away.

Dad's Lavallette house was awesome in the summer and early fall, but the winters were harsh, and they vowed to never spend another winter on the beach. When my dad was working on a new novel, he liked to surround himself with an area that matches the location of the book. That's what brought Dad and Sara to Belvidere, New Jersey, a quaint Victorian town near the Delaware Water Gap. Moving here was like stepping back in time, especially this time of year, the Christmas holidays.

That's when things get magical, even more than usual. Of course, anything Sara engages in gets magical, laughable, or both at some point. A couple of months before turning eighteen, I chose to live only with my dad. It's not that I don't love my mom, but ever since she married Chris, I rarely saw her. I would wander through their enormous home—too clean thanks to Monica, who came weekly even when no one was there to step on the vacuum tracks left the week prior. I felt so much more loved and wanted with my dad and Sara. So I sat everyone down together and announced that I wanted to live with Dad full-time until I could afford my own place.

"Are you sure, Danielle?" my mother asked, just a little too brightly.

"Mom. You are always traveling somewhere, and I get bored being alone all the time."

"Well, I guess it's up to your father, then."

My dad's head snapped up, and he corrected her quickly. "And Sara."

"My mistake. Your father and Sara." My mother's voice had a hint of sarcasm on the "and." "If that's what will make you happy, then you have my blessing."

I felt like my mom agreed a little too easily and a bit too quickly, but she can be like that.

Dad and Sara looked at each other and, somehow in unison, said, "Dani, we would love to have you live with us."

Sara clapped her hands, and my dad got tears in his eyes (which happens a lot lately).

That went a lot better than the next few minutes, when I added that not only was I moving out of my mom's place, I also didn't want to go to college. At least not right away after graduating high school.

My mother likes to raise her eyebrows and give me "the look" whenever she's displeased, but she'd just had Botox injections, and she couldn't do that. I tried not to laugh as I watched her eyes get big but without her eyebrows moving.

Dad had a confused look on his face, but he didn't seem angry or disappointed. Sara reached over to rub my arm with a small smile.

My dad ran his hands through his still thick but graying hair. "Dani, are you sure about this? I thought we were on the same page. Community college for two years and then transfer for your bachelor's degree."

"I'm super sure, Dad. I've been thinking about this for months. I don't want to go. Honestly, I've been shuffling back and forth for so long. I just want to put down roots, stay in one spot, and work for a year."

Sara rubbed my arm again. "Maybe a year's wait isn't a bad idea, especially if you feel you're not ready."

She gets me, and even if she doesn't, she cares enough to try.

"Sara, while your input may endear you to my daughter, this is something Erik and I should deal with." Mom added a small, pinched smile to her words so it wouldn't sound harsh. Unfortunately, it still came off that way, and Sara's eyebrows did the thing my mom's couldn't.

"I wouldn't think of interfering, Cynthia. But if Dani is going to live with us full-time, I think my input is valid and needed."

I watched my mother's face, and I knew she was desperately trying to give Sara "the look." Sara looked back at her and raised just one eyebrow. Then she raised the other one. And then she smiled her biggest smile and said, "Let's figure out what the next year is going to look like."

And that's exactly how we ended up owning a very quaint bookstore in the very quaint town of Belvidere.

The bell tinkled Sara's return, bringing me back to the present. We hooked arms and walked to the little kitchenette we'd set up in the back room of the shop to drink coffee and catch up.

CHAPTER 2

SARA

I sipped the delicious coffee and thanked Dani with a smile and a tip of my huge mug. It's my second favorite one (my favorite lives at home). For me, it's all in the handle and how my hand feels wrapped around it. That could apply to my mugs *and* to my future husband. That realization made me do a giggle/choke thing, and coffee is not as wonderful when it comes out of your nose.

"Sara, you're all red, are you okay?"

"I'm"—*cough*—"fine." There was no way I was going to share what made me choke with Dani. We already get enough eye rolls and "ewwwws" to last a lifetime. Erik and I were just as gooey now as we were at the beginning of our relationship. "Before I fill you in on our trip, tell me about your week. You saw Tristan?"

Tristan was Dani's on-again, off-again boyfriend. They met shortly after Erik and I did, also at the beach, and then spent the summer deeply in love, as only a seventeen-year-old girl can be with a nineteen-year-old boy. Over the past eighteen months, they'd taken a few breaks from the relationship, but the time spent apart seemed to prove the adage "absence makes the heart grow fonder" and they'd reconcile.

"Yeah. Yesterday, we went out for Thai and then hung out with the dogs and watched TV," Dani said with a hint of boredom.

"Are you guys heading for another break?" With Dani, boredom always meant something was going to change.

Dani twirled a chunk of her blond hair and shook her head. "No… I don't know. Things are okay right now. I don't know what I want when it comes to him. We have a great time together usually. But I feel like I'm too young to settle down with my first 'real' boyfriend. Plus, it takes over an hour for one of us to drive to the other."

Tristan lived with his mother and her wife close to Philadelphia, where Lisa and Rachel owned a successful antiques and collectibles shop. He went to college part-time while working at their shop. He had very little spare time to devote to a girlfriend over an hour away, yet they kept returning to the relationship. I am well beyond trying to understand anyone else's feelings, and I just made sure I was there for Dani whenever she needed an ear to listen or a shoulder to cry on.

The bell on the door tinkled an arrival, and I motioned to Dani to stay seated while I saw to the customer. Only it wasn't a customer, it was a delivery. The box was so big it obscured the driver's face, and he struggled to look around it. He froze mid-step right before he would have fallen over a box of unpacked books near the counter.

"Let me help you!" I grabbed an end, and we lowered it to the ground together.

"Sorry about that! I was doing fine carrying it until I got inside the shop and then suddenly, I wasn't fine. It was so strange, I felt like I was being stopped somehow." The delivery driver shook his head as if to shake off a brain fog that had overtaken him.

He was young, extremely cute, and unfamiliar to me.

"No worries. Glad I could help. Are you new on our route or

just helping for the holidays?" I asked him, all the while mentally willing Dani to come out and see this guy.

Hey. Come out here. Cute guy alert.

Dani and I had this thing where I always knew when a text from her would come in seconds before my phone alerted me. Or I'd feel something was off and sure enough, Dani would text venting about whatever upset her at that moment. But instead of Dani, I saw our cat, Kat, peering around a bookshelf, staring intensely at the stranger.

"New to you. I've been delivering for a couple of years, but this is my new route. Cole." He stuck out his gloved hand and I shook it and introduced myself.

"Nice to meet you. My name is Sara. I own the shop with my bonus daughter, Dani." I said the Dani part more loudly than the rest of my sentence, hoping she'd take the damn hint already. "You'll be delivering here pretty often. Between books, coffee, and other oddities coming in, we're usually a steady stop."

I smiled at Cole, and he smiled back. Good teeth. I always notice the teeth. That's what decades of working in a dental office will do to you. Nice lips too. I'd guess early twenties. The uniform enhanced rather than detracted from his build, which was easy to look at. I wondered if I was taking a little too much inventory, but I argued back to myself that it was all for Dani's sake if she didn't get her butt out here to see for herself.

"Well, I'd better get back to work. At this rate, I'm going to be working some overtime." He flashed a handsome grin. "I am not complaining about that. Glad for the extra money." With a wave, he turned to go, and before I could think of something else to keep him there, he was gone.

"Who was that?" Dani came around the corner, wiping her hands with a paper towel.

"Just the cutest delivery guy ever."

"Why didn't you come get me?" she asked with a laugh.

"I tried sending you one of our mental messages. You must have your receiver off."

"Dammit. I was cleaning the litter box, so my mind was on crap, literally."

A husky meow that sounded more like hello came from Kat, our resident cat, who had adopted us after we signed the lease on the shop.

"I don't know who it belongs to." The landlord had shrugged. "Never saw it before. Showed up this morning very insistent on coming in. I was here doing a last walk-through before you signed, and it followed me right in." He jerked his thumb at the door. "Just throw the damn thing outside before you leave. You never know what kind of mess it'll make."

The cat had hissed and glared at him with bright green eyes, as if it knew what he said.

I did the exact opposite of throwing the cat out. Dani ran to the market next to Charms for cat litter and food. I took her to the vet right away, and she checked out perfectly. The only unusual thing about her was the section of hair growing out of the top of her head between her ears. It was longer than the rest of her coat. She was all black, but that section was white. Pure white.

The doctor gently stroked the long hair growing between the cat's ears. "You don't see this type of coat very often. If you ever want to do a DNA test on her, let me know."

A low growl came out of the cat's throat, so I told him I'd think about it and let him know. It didn't seem like she was a fan of the idea.

We named her Kat, and she's been with us ever since. When she's not guarding the shop, Kat sleeps on a fluffy pillow in the front window and expects customers to pay homage. Molly will sometimes come to work with me and try to play with her, but Kat never tolerates it. She'll jump up on a shelf where Molly has no chance of reaching her. Then she twitches her tail, showing her annoyance, and glares at every human walking past.

"So, he was cute, huh?"

"Yup. Nice build too."

"Dammit. Is he temporary for the holidays?"

"No, he's permanent. So you'll get plenty of opportunities to see him."

Dani rolled her eyes. "Just what I need to complicate my life."

I laughed. "How complicated is your life?"

"Well, you know. The whole Tristan thing. It's complicated."

Dani had no idea what complicated looked like. I thought back to the day Erik had proposed to me, when we were navigating the effects of a massive storm while harboring my ex-husband and our hussy of a neighbor shoving her tatas in Erik's face.

CHAPTER 3

DANI

After Sara finished her coffee and washed the mugs, she left to go back home and unpack. I looked around at the work to be done and attacked the boxes of books and tarot cards waiting to be stocked. When I finally came up for air, I noticed that not only had the sun gone down, but it was also time to lock the door and call it a day. Stocking shelves with the chapter part of Charms & Chapters was easy, the charms part not so much. Tarot cards and books, wands, crystals and other witchy items needed more attention to placement.

I changed the Open sign to Closed and flipped the lock. Pulling the shade down, I noticed the snow-covered sidewalk. I walked to work this morning, and I was grateful it was only a few short blocks to get home because I'd forgotten my snow boots.

I texted Sara, letting her know I'd be walking home after feeding Kat. She answered with an offer to pick me up, but I told her I'd be fine. It would only take me a few minutes to get home.

"Kat, food?" I called out.

She came running from her spot on the pillow, skidding as she reached the luncheonette. Meowing her hello, she serpentined between my legs. I swore she was trying to trip me. They'll find me with a can of salmon pâté gripped tightly in my hand—half empty because she'd probably eat what she could off my cold, dead body.

Absent-mindedly, I watched her eat, my brain filled with everything I wanted to get done before Christmas. I had a few presents left to buy, but both Sara and I made most of our gifts this year. I loved making art with her. She let me use her supplies any time I wanted. This year we made Christmas trees out of sea glass glued to driftwood. Thanks to the daily walks we used to take on the beach in Lavallette, we had a huge supply of both. Sara got more glue on herself than driftwood, but at least she's good-natured about it. Honestly, I think she's used to it.

A raspy greeting brought me back to the present. Kat rubbed her face on my socks, essentially using me as her napkin, and then trotted off to her litter box.

"Not again." I moaned. "Didn't I just take care of all that?"

I texted Sara an update so she wouldn't worry.

DANI

Kat is pooping again. Leaving as soon as I clean the box.

SARA

Oh, no! Thanks for staying and doing that. That would have been ripe in the morning.

DANI

Seriously. Bad enough right now.

Sara returned the puking emoji, which was about how I was feeling. Kat finished her business and got the zoomies, tearing around the shop.

I finished cleaning up while Kat zoomed. Pulling on my coat, I peeked out the window and, of course, it had snowed almost an inch in the short time since I'd locked up and was still coming down. Looking down at my old black Converse sneakers, I resigned myself to wet feet and locked the door behind me.

As I pulled my key from the lock, I felt myself slide down the ever so slightly inclined cement ramp leading towards the sidewalk. Backwards. My heels hit the bottom of the ramp, and the sudden stop threw me down onto the sidewalk.

I lay there for a second while the wind came back into my lungs.

"Are you okay? That looks like it hurt."

My brain heard the male voice, and it wasn't the cold air causing my cheeks to flame with embarrassment. Sara must be rubbing off on me.

"I think so." I sat up and tried to get my footing, but my sneakers were worse than ice skates and I landed again, this time twisting my left ankle. Tears sprang to my eyes, and I gasped. "Wait. I take that back."

"Let me help you up. See if you can put any weight on it," the voice continued. "Here, I'm going to lift you."

I'd yet to see my hero. He was behind me, and the falling snow dimmed the streetlights. I felt his hands slide under my armpits and he lifted me like I was a feather.

"Okay, now put your foot down and see if you can stand. I won't let go yet."

I tried to put weight on it, but it hurt, and judging by the tightness of my sneaker, it was already swelling.

"I can't." I felt his hands grip me a little tighter, and I turned my head as far as I could to see his face.

The light was dim, and the snow sticking to my eyelashes made it difficult to make out details, but from what I could see, he was hot. Tall, dark, and handsome might sound cliché, but it applied here. I was guessing this was the new delivery guy Sara had told me about. He felt me turn in his arms and gripped my shoulders instead of my armpits.

"Careful. I don't want you falling again." There was a smile in his voice.

I looked up at him. Dark eyes. Great mouth. His coat hid most of his body, but it felt good pressed up against me. I shivered as the cold, wet ground soaked through my sneakers.

"Where's your car? Can you drive? Is there someone you can call to help?"

All those questions flew from his mouth as he looked around the empty street for my vehicle.

"No, I walked." A little sob escaped from my throat. "I can call my dad or stepmom. We live just a couple of blocks up the road. I'll just go back to the shop to wait."

"I'm not going to leave you until someone comes. I can't drive you home myself; not allowed to have anyone except employees in the truck." He bit his lip, his very full, not at all chapped lip. "Or maybe I could just carry you to your house."

With that, he put his right arm around my shoulders, his left behind my knees, and up in the air I went.

"No! Seriously! Put me down, you don't have to marry me. Oh my God, I mean carry me." I laughed to cover my embarrassment.

He quickly put my feet gently on the ground but kept his right arm around my shoulders. "I could have done it, you know," he said with a wink.

Which thing could he have done?

His dark eyes were mesmerizing, and our lips were ohsoclose. Sara wasn't exaggerating. Chiseled face, high cheekbones, and those amazing eyes and why were my lips chapped when his were so freaking smooth?

I chewed my chapped bottom lip until I saw his eyes drop to my lips. I abruptly stopped, but his eyes stayed on my lips, sending butterflies into my belly, among other places. Slowly, his left hand reached into his coat pocket and pulled out a tube of lip balm. His eyes met mine as he expertly flipped open the cap with one hand and slid it across his lips.

"Want to try some? I got it at the store up the street. Works great."

His lips were a testament to how well it worked. Also, the thought crossed my mind that I should never use a stranger's lip balm. But I was getting ready to kiss him so that balm would get on my lips anyway. And with that thought, I went up on my toes on my good foot and pressed my cold, chapped lips to his.

I did not know who or what made me do it, but it was just as delicious as I expected. Dad always said "expectations lead to disappointment" but I was not disappointed in the least.

"Sorry! I don't know what came over me!" I started laughing because this kind of thing never happened to me. There was a small twinge of guilt when I realized Tristan had never even crossed my mind before I gave into what felt like an urge I couldn't control.

"Don't apologize. If you hadn't, I probably would have. Maybe I should introduce myself. I'm Cole and I'm on your route now, assuming you're Sara's daughter?" He paused. "I saw you locking up so just assuming."

"Yes. Stepdaughter, but she's like a mom to me. I'm Danielle. Dani."

"You're lucky. Many people can't say that. She seemed cool when I met her earlier. You weren't around."

"No." I laughed. "I was cleaning the litter box for our cat, Kat. Fun times."

"You call your cat Cat?"

"Yes, but with a K, so people say it correctly."

He was adorable when he was confused.

I suddenly realized I would not make it back up that slight incline to the front door of our shop without hurting something else.

"Would you be able to get me inside the shop?" I giggled at the absurdity of the previous five minutes. Had it only been five minutes? Time seemed to stand still. His arms were still holding me up, strong and steady. And why was I giggling?

"Give me your keys and show me which one is for this door." Cole made it up the ramp without issue, leaving me standing in the still falling snow, just a few feet away. He unlocked the door and propped it open.

Turning back to me, he scooped me up in his arms again and carried me over the threshold into the shop.

Carried me over the threshold.

Before he put me down, he looked into my eyes. Deep into my eyes. Like he was looking into my brain and seeing flashes of wedding dresses and bridesmaids with large pink satin bows on their butts.

Breaking the moment, he gently put me down and helped me to a chair in the reading area just inside the door. Cole knelt in front of me and, before I could protest, he slipped off my soaking wet sneaker and pulled off my equally wet sock. I shivered, but not entirely from my cold, wet feet. His hands held my foot, and he gently pressed all around my ankle.

"Your foot is like ice, but that might have actually helped." Cole let go of my foot and looked up at me. "See how it feels tomorrow. You might need to see a doctor."

"Thank you for all this, for helping me and everything. I need to let my stepmom know what's happening and why I'm not home yet." I sent Sara a text briefly explaining my predicament and turned my attention back to Cole, who had started walking to the door.

"I've got to get back to the hub, but I'm still willing to carry you home if you'll let me."

I felt a warmth shoot through my body as I imagined his arms around me again. I focused my eyes on his lips, so soft, so kissable. That warmth? It got warmer. My ankle practically forgotten, I stood to answer him so that I could be closer to his lips.

And then I kissed him. Again. What the hell, girl? What are you doing? Again!

In the split second after my lips broke away from his, two

things happened. Kat started hissing and spitting, and Sara and Dad walked in.

CHAPTER 4

SARA

I was in the kitchen reading Dani's "help me" text when Erik came in. "Good timing. Dani needs help getting home. She slipped on some ice and hurt her ankle."

"I'll go get her. Wanna come along for the road trip?" Erik chuckled, since it was so close.

I slipped my feet into boots, shrugged on a coat, and followed him out the front door. "The porch looks amazing! You got so much done already." Erik had spent the afternoon decorating the front porch for Christmas. He'd strung colorful lights, and real fir boughs wrapped each post and railing. I knew he was far from done, and I could tell how much fun he was having designing his masterpiece, though he wouldn't admit it.

"Your creativity is wearing off on me, Sara." He smiled, yet he still looked surprised and impressed with how beautiful it looked.

The snow was falling lightly as we walked to Erik's four-wheel drive SUV. We backed out onto Main Street and drove the two blocks to the bookshop. The delivery truck was parked in front, and I wondered if Cole and Dani had met. Erik pulled a U-turn on the empty street and parked behind the truck.

I got both feet securely under me so I wouldn't end up like Dani, and no sooner had that thought gone through my brain than I ended up on the ground just like Dani.

"Sara! Babe! You okay?" Erik hooked his hands under my arms and lifted me to my feet.

"I think so. That happened so fast I couldn't stop myself! But, yeah, I think I'm intact."

Erik chuckled and held my hand as we entered the shop. Dani and Cole were standing very close, and Kat was grousing and hissing, her tail switching violently back and forth as she watched them. Dani's face was pink, her eyes wide and her lips pursed, looking startled by our sudden appearance.

Erik rapid-fired questions immediately. "Dani? Are you all right? What's going on here? Who is this?"

Kat answered before Dani could, hissing and spitting at Cole.

"Dad! This is Cole," Dani sputtered, her face still flushed. "He saw me fall. He was just helping me."

Erik looked Cole up and down, his face unreadable.

"Sir, I apologize. I was just coming around the corner when I saw her fall. I helped her inside, and that's all."

Cole's face appeared earnest, and his words seemed to satisfy Erik, but I kept my eyes on Dani, and an entirely different version of the story appeared in my head. I could feel the energy between her and Cole. Dani's blush told me there was more to this, and I was looking forward to hearing it from her when we were alone.

"Is your ankle ok?" I asked. "How bad is the pain? Can you walk on it?"

Dani seemed grateful for the change of topic and sat down. "It hurts, but not as bad as a few minutes ago. Please don't make me go to urgent care. I'm sure I'll be fine tomorrow."

"Let me look." Erik bent down to look at Dani's ankle. "It's a bit swollen and there's already some bruising. Let's get some ice on it when we get home, and we'll make that decision tomorrow."

I looked at Cole, who was moving towards the front door.

"Cole, thank you so much for helping her. You were in the right place at the right time."

"Hey, I'm glad I was right here." A hiss from Kat at that moment made Cole's brow furrow briefly. "I have to get back to the hub, but I'll probably stop in tomorrow to check even if you have no deliveries."

Another hiss/growl combination from Kat moved him more quickly to the door. He waved and disappeared into the snowy night.

CHAPTER 5

DANI

I watched Cole leave the shop, and my brain started playing a slideshow of the past fifteen minutes. Me slipping on the icy sidewalk, Cole's arms, Cole's lips, our two kisses, Kat freaking out, Dad walking in on us. The feeling of shame, tinged with embarrassment at my totally out-of-character impulses, washed over me and pushed down the ache of what I could only call pure lust. But almost getting caught by my dad took the wind out of those sails.

Luckily, I think Dad was more concerned about my ankle than what was going on with Cole. But one glance at Sara told me she was intensely curious about what had happened, and I had to laugh at how connected we were. It still caught me off guard.

"I didn't think to bring your snow boots," Sara said. "How are we going to get you into Dad's car?"

"I can hop," I said with more confidence than I felt.

"Sure, you can." Dad chuckled. "And sprain both ankles."

With that, he scooped me up in his arms and asked Sara to wait for him to come back for her, just to be safe. When we got to the car, I pulled the back door open and Dad gently draped me across the back seat.

Once he had also escorted Sara to the car without another incident, we carefully slid the two blocks home and Dad piggybacked me into the house.

"The porch is amazing! You two got so much done this afternoon!" Just looking at the Christmas lights wrapped around the pine boughs made me forget about my ankle.

"Didn't he do a great job?" Sara's face showed how proud she was of her fiancé. "I can't take any credit. Your dad did all of this while I unpacked and started laundry."

"I'm impressed." I laughed. "He's good with words, but this kind of stuff? No way."

My father bent his knees quickly, like he was going to drop me. "Watch it, kiddo. You're on dangerous ground." He turned his face towards me so I could see his eyes were twinkling, and I knew he'd never drop me. On purpose, anyway.

After dodging both dogs, he gently put me down into a kitchen chair and checked my ankle over again. "I know your foot is freezing right now, but it's probably helping to keep the swelling down."

Cole had said those same words earlier. Cole. My insides squirmed again at the thought of him.

"I'm going to put an ice pack on it, anyway," Dad continued. "And then I'll wrap it with that good stuff I got from Lucas." Lucas is our friend and neighbor, and a physical therapist associated with a nearby gym.

The kitchen was warm and cozy, with beautiful wood floors and cabinets but I loved the tin ceiling best of all. My dad was determined to remodel and update the countertop and cabinets, but Sara made him promise he wouldn't touch the ceiling. A slow cooker filled with something that smelled delicious simmered on the counter.

I shrugged out of my coat as my dad wrapped an ice pack around my ankle.

"I'm just securing it temporarily, and I want you to sit for twenty minutes."

"Can I pee?"

My dad rolled his eyes. "You could have mentioned that before I got done."

"Can you carry me, Daddy?" I said in a squeaky little voice.

He burst out laughing and crouched down in front of my chair so I could climb on his back.

He grunted. "This was a lot easier when you were four." He laughed and dumped me cautiously in front of the toilet. "This is as far as I go. Yell for Sara if you require any further accommodation."

"I'm good, Dad. I can manage it." I waved him away. When I finished and opened the door, I found him crouched down ready to piggyback me back to a chair.

"Your chariot awaits, My Lady."

"Thank you, Daddy," I said in that same squeaky voice and got a chuckle in response.

Sara was dishing out sourdough bread bowls full of chili, and my stomach growled as my father sat me down again gently in my chair. She gave me a raised eyebrow when she set my bowl in front of me. Not a word was spoken, but that look let me know she still had questions brewing. Lots of them, no doubt.

CHAPTER 6

SARA

I wasn't about to grill Dani about Cole with her dad sitting next to her. There was no way she would tell me the complete story unless we were alone. Erik cleaned up after dinner before carrying Dani upstairs to her room.

"We thought a Victorian was a good idea because…?" Erik grumbled when he was halfway up to the second floor.

"Be thankful my bedroom isn't in the attic, like it was in the Pendleton." Dani laughed in his ear. "You never would have gotten me up those death stairs."

This was no exaggeration. The stairs leading to the attic really were hazardous, which is why we called them the death stairs, and I rarely made my way up there. Not a soul in this world would want to see my clumsy butt climbing up or down those steps. But when we first moved in, I had heard there was a witches' chimney, and I had to go check it out. Shortly after I met Erik, I encountered a mysterious woman in Lavallette named Lily. And ever since she did an impromptu but life-changing tarot reading with me, I'd been exploring tarot, the craft, and various Wiccan and pagan customs. It was all fascinating and resonated with me in a way organized religion never had. Some of that changing belief system had certainly worked its way into our bookshop as well.

Upon discovering the chimney here and surviving my one trip up and down the death stairs, I did some research. Turns out it's called a witches' chimney, witches' crook, or witches' bend because the chimney itself takes a slight turn. Based on an old wives' tale, people believed witches could fly only in straight lines, so with the bend, they could not access your home through your chimney.

I have to laugh at that because I walk through the kitchen door like any other self-respecting witch.

Erik was coming downstairs as I started going up and we paused when I got one step above him to make out a little. That one step meant I didn't have to get up on my tiptoes to reach his mouth. My lips hit his. The same sparks that flew during our very first kiss still flew every time. His hands ran up and down my back and settled on my bra, where he tried to unclasp the unforgiving hooks.

"I hate bras. Why do you even wear one? You're home. Nobody's coming over." Erik growled in my ear. "And dammit, I can't unhook it."

"Well, I was on my way to change into jammies and do just that, but you interrupted me by passing me here with your fine self."

"Hey, can you guys stop your old people sex talk for one second and bring me my phone?" Dani called from her room at the top of the stairs. "I think I left it in the kitchen."

"The owner never mentioned the thin walls when he showed us this house," I said. "Stop calling us old!"

I heard Dani's chuckle through the wall next to our heads.

"I'm really glad our room is at the other end of the house," I whispered to Erik.

"Me too," Dani called out.

"I'll go get it," Erik offered. "You continue doing what you were doing before I distracted you with my bad self." His wolf smile appeared, and he rubbed a thumb across the front of my shirt-covered bra. "Hurry."

"GUYS!" Dani yelled. "Please!"

Laughing, I continued my climb to our bedroom, and Erik headed down to look for Dani's phone. I peeked into her room before heading down the hall, since the door was open.

"You know I have a million questions, right?"

Dani laughed and turned pink. "I know. And I want to tell you all about it. But I don't want Dad to hear."

"Dad hears everything." Erik's voice came from outside her door. "Here's your phone, kiddo. What answers wouldn't you want me to hear?"

"Dad, it's girl stuff. I need Sara."

Erik tossed Dani's phone on her bed and huffed out of the room. "I'm in touch with my feminine side. I don't know why you don't realize that."

Dani and I exchanged a grin and a roll of the eyes.

"I'll be there in a bit, babe!" I called out to his retreating back and shut Dani's door behind me.

I kept my voice low. "Spill it. I could feel the energy coming off the two of you in the shop. It was electric. Did something happen? Did you kiss? He's got great lips. When I was checking out his teeth, I couldn't help but notice the lips. So?"

Dani sucked a quick breath in and started spilling. "I have no freaking idea what came over me with him. He's got some kind of vibe that is just... like it sucks you in and you can't think of anything else. He helped me up off the sidewalk and his hands were on fire through my coat." Dani paused, chewing her lip. "I couldn't stop myself and I kissed him. I kissed him, Sara. I never even thought about Tristan. How could I do that? And then I did it again inside the shop. And again, I never thought about Tristan."

I saw tears spring to her eyes as a guilty look came over her face.

"Do I tell him? Tristan? Do I tell him what I did? Or do I just file it away in some folder in my brain and try to forget it ever happened? And I'll probably end up seeing Cole every day at Charms, so how will I ever forget? Am I going to jump into his arms every time I see him?" Dani's voice grew more panicky with each word.

I grabbed her hand. "Breathe. You're fine. You're safe. Let's talk about this more tomorrow when you've had a good night's sleep and it's not so fresh. Okay? I got my initial questions answered. Tomorrow we'll work through it bit by bit and figure out what your next step should be."

I gave her a quick hug and said good night.

"Thanks, Sara. Hey, can Molly sleep with me tonight?"

"Of course." I called for my golden retriever and heard her paws coming up the stairs. I patted the bed and Molly jumped up and at once made herself comfortable next to Dani. "Don't blame me when she snores. You asked for this."

Dani tried to position herself against seventy pounds of fur and clucked her tongue. "We'll be fine. Right, Molly?"

Molly didn't answer; she was already snoring.

CHAPTER 7

DANI

After Sara left, I grabbed my phone and searched social media for Cole. Nothing. A last name would have helped. I wondered if asking for his last name would be too forward but then remembered that I'd kissed him twice, so maybe not.

A bolt of shame hit my belly. Where was this guilt when I had kissed Cole? I remembered staring at his lips and the discussion of his lip balm and then, without another thought, I had kissed him. I shook my head and took Sara's advice just to go to sleep. The pain relievers were doing their job, along with the excellent wrap job my dad did on my ankle.

I put my phone on DND, buried my face in Molly's soft coat, and promptly fell into a dreamless sleep.

Molly's kisses woke me and made me smile. The golden retriever smiled back at me and thumped her tail on the bed. It was early, only 7:30 a.m., but my alarm would go off shortly. Turning it off before it could, I threw back the covers and set my feet on the floor. "Test run," I said out loud to Molly. "Let's see if this ankle is going to work."

Surprisingly, it didn't feel horrible. I walked to my bedroom door and could put almost full weight on it. Feeling relieved, I made my way to the bathroom across the hall.

Sara and I usually took turns opening and closing Charms & Chapters, except with her and Dad being gone for the past week I'd been tasked with both. Since I hadn't talked to her about who would open today, I got ready. That Cole might deliver to us early had nothing to do with that decision.

I regretted not showering last night, but there was no way my ankle would have held me. Molly left the room, padding down the hall to Dad and Sara's room. Their door was still closed, so she made her way downstairs to see if there was any action in the kitchen. Tank would be at the bottom of the stairs waiting for her, just like he was every morning. His legs were too short for the steep stairs, so Tank became King of the First Floor.

After showering and brushing my teeth, inspecting every pore, and banishing some stray eyebrow hairs, I returned to my room to get dressed. Pulling out black yoga pants and a gray hoodie, I posed in front of my full-length mirror and judged myself. It looked like something Sara would wear, but that didn't bother me. I loved the way Sara dressed. She always looked good, and she always looked comfortable. Sara said life was too short for tight pants. I agreed mostly, but I love my vintage low-rise bell-bottom jeans. Sara had found them for me in a shop in New Hope last year, and I wear the hell out of them.

I bet Cole would like those.

I've learned to listen to my inner voice, so I slowly stripped off the yoga pants and pulled the jeans from my drawer. Inspecting myself once again, I decided the hoodie didn't show off the low-risers, so off it came. A form-fitting long-sleeved T-shirt in camo green completed the outfit.

I was resigned to blow-drying my hair, which incidentally gave it a little more lift than when I let it dry naturally, because there was no way I was going out in the frigid morning air with a wet head. I told myself that lie and almost believed it, but I'd frozen my hair so many times this month already it was clearly bullshit. I wanted fluffy waves for Cole. The little mascara swipe was for Cole, too. And the pink lip gloss. The moss agate wire-wrapped necklace I got for my birthday. Yes. For Cole. All for Cole, a guy I barely knew, had already kissed twice, and could not get out of my head.

My dad's voice followed a knock on the bedroom door. "Dani, do you need any help?"

"No, Dad, it feels pretty good this morning!" I called out, and opened the door to show him how well I could walk.

"Look at you all dolled up so early. Is Tristan coming up today?"

"No, I just felt like wearing my favorite jeans." My face flushed at Tristan's name and with the lie. Of course, my dad noticed.

He looked at me quizzically, taking in the hair, mascara, and lip gloss. I used to wear lots of makeup, but Sara had shown me a more natural look, and I rarely wore any makeup at all anymore.

He chuckled and shook his head. "I'm guessing this is another Sara subject, so I'll just head downstairs and cook some bacon. You want eggs or pancakes?"

Dad was already heading to the door planning his menu, and I called out "pancakes!" to his retreating back. He threw me a thumbs-up as he started down the stairs.

I pushed myself away from the kitchen table, gripping my stomach and groaning. Why did I eat so many pancakes? And the bacon? Although I read somewhere that the smell of bacon was an aphrodisiac for guys. My stomach would have been happier if I'd just rubbed the crispy crackly deliciousness directly on my abdomen.

An image of Cole sniffing my abdomen sent a lightning strike between my legs. I wondered if there was any leftover bacon on the counter. Neither dog had left their posts next to Dad's chair and empty plate, so I doubted it.

"I ate way too much." I sighed. "Maybe the yoga pants would have been a better choice."

"How's your ankle? Let me see your outfit!" Sara appeared in the kitchen wearing her loungewear. That's what Sara calls them, anyway. She said they look like jogging suits from the '80s, only soft and stretchy.

"It feels pretty good!" I said with a happy smile. "I'm so glad I don't have to go to urgent care." I stood up to show Sara what I was wearing.

She nodded with her approval. "What shoes are you going to pair with that?"

"Probably my black combat boots. They have a good tread and will support my ankle."

Sara nodded approval again, yawned, and poured a mug of coffee from the waiting pot. "I'm thankful you're ready to open. I didn't sleep well last night." And then she gave my father a very pointed look and raised her eyebrow.

I put my forehead down on the table. "Please. Can we at least stay away from old people sex talk at the table?" I said it with a joking, disgusted tone. But honestly, I was glad my dad was so happy. Life was now divided into "Before Sara" and "After Sara."

"After Sara" is a much better world for me and my dad. "After Sara" is filled with love, laughter, and a world painted in color. And magic. I was glad they were finally going to get married.

My dad smirked, said "Make me," and stuck his tongue out.

I rolled my eyes in return and got up to get my boots. "You guys are so mature. Are you coming in at all today, Sara?"

"I am. I promise to be there by 11:00. I'll pack us a lunch. Sound good?"

I made a mental note to have a fresh pot of coffee ready for

11:00 a.m. We have a full coffee and tea setup in the back room. It's nothing fancy, but our customers know the coffee is always on, with basic additions like cream and sugar. Tea is an option, with old standbys like Earl Grey and English Breakfast. Lots of our regulars come in to browse new book selections, pottery, and witchy items, all while sipping a hot beverage. And paying attention to Molly or Kat, of course. The two fur babies practically owned the place. No one seemed to mind the fluff. You had to expect a cat or dog hair puffball on the old wood plank floors. We're talking golden retriever hair; there's nothing quite like it.

"Sounds like a plan. Thanks. PB&J if you're taking requests." I called the last part from the dining room door as I left to walk to work.

I applauded my boot choice as I made my way down the slushy sidewalk. I also gave myself props for tucking my pants inside them. Sara had long ago warned me against the dangers of dragging the bell bottoms on the ground.

The day was sunny and the little snow we had ended up with was melting quickly. I pulled my aviator sunglasses from my small purse and grabbed the shop keys at the same time. The walk wasn't long, and it brought me past the three storefronts that preceded ours on the block: An art gallery/gift shop filled with cool and quirky items handmade by local artisans. A vintage record shop, which my dad said was the main reason they bought this house. An amazing Thai restaurant was our direct neighbor and a great option on nights we didn't feel like cooking. Just past the shop was a small market that carried excellent cuts of beef, another favorite of my dad's.

I carefully tested my footing as I approached the front door to Charms & Chapters, and it felt safe to put the key in the lock.

"Don't fall."

Startled by Cole's voice from behind me, I dropped my keys and cursed softly.

"I'm so sorry. Let me get them for you."

Cole bent down on one knee in front of me, and yes, my mind went there. He handed the keys to me and smiled, still on his knee on the wet sidewalk. "I didn't mean to scare you. Can you forgive me? How's your ankle, by the way? You seem to be walking without a limp."

Get off your knee, Cole, unless you mean business. I shushed the voice in my head. "My ankle feels so much better. These boots give it a lot of support. And no worries. I startle easily."

My heart was pounding, and I could feel my cheeks burning just standing next to him. Whatever pheromones he was selling, my body was buying. I let myself have a moment and just take him in. All logic left my brain when he was nearby. His dark hair was thick and cut short. A bit of curl beginning to show. Clean-shaven. Those fabulous cheekbones. Dark eyes, a deep hazel brown that caught the morning sunlight exactly right. Everything about him was exactly right. Especially his lips.

I should kiss him good morning. When that thought popped into my head, honestly, it took everything in my power to stop myself.

I shook my head to clear my brain of all the things I wanted to do with Cole.

"Thanks again for last night. I don't know what I would have done if you weren't in the right place at the right time."

"It was totally my pleasure." Cole grinned, showing off his gorgeous teeth and those dang lips. "I know I have stuff on the truck for you, but I need to deliver the overnights first. I'll be back this afternoon."

Cole waited until I successfully let myself into Charms & Chapters without calamity. I waved goodbye and looked around the shop, shaking my head at the mess we'd left on the old wood floors last night. I relocked the door behind me since we wouldn't open for another half hour. Wiping my feet good on the area rug inside the door, I started for the tiny kitchenette to grab something to clean up the water stains and salty slush. Kat was waiting in there, giving me a rather judgmental side-eye as she tapped her empty food bowl with her front paw.

"Allow me to prioritize you, Kat," I said with a bit of sarcasm as I filled her kibble bowl. Happy with fresh water and food, Kat purred and wrapped herself around my ankles. Luckily, I had a mop in my hands to support myself and keep me from falling as Kat walked perfect figure eights between my feet.

I bent down and scratched her behind the ears, her favorite spot. "Why did you hiss at Cole last night? Hmmmm?"

Kat stopped purring and turned to look me in the eye. Her gaze was mesmerizing. I almost forgot she was a cat. That's how startling it was. Then she sneezed and started cleaning her paws, ignoring me while I cleaned up last night's mess and readied the shop for opening.

Colorful bohemian lamps hung above the small reading area to the right of the front door, and I turned each one on, creating a warm glow over the comfortable chairs and tables. It was the perfect spot to enjoy a hot drink and relax with a book.

The lighting was more direct over the bookshelves at the back of the shop, allowing customers to read book jackets and peruse the tarot card decks and crystals that dotted the shelves alongside the books. Kat had knocked nothing off the shelves lately, something she had liked to do when we first got her. We'd come into the room and there would be rocks, crystals, and various oddities strewn across the floor. Kat would be sitting in the middle of it all, her eyes slitted and her tail twitching. Unapologetic, of course.

I was dusting the shelves when there was a knock on the door. I peeked out the window since we were technically still closed for five more minutes. Lorelei, the owner of the art gallery, waved at me.

"Let me in! It's freezing out here!"

I unlocked the door, and she practically fell into the shop, breathless and stomping her feet on the entry rug. Lorelei's long black hair was braided and pulled up on the top of her head. She wore a multicolored flowing dress and a pair of wellies. No coat. No wonder she was freezing.

"Dani. Tell me you've met the new delivery guy. He's amazing."

Lorelei was twenty-three and gorgeous. Although her parents technically owned the gallery, Lorelei ran the day-to-day business. They had little involvement and very little say. She lived in the apartment above her shop. We were friendly but didn't hang out. I envied her, done with college and running a successful gallery by herself, and here I was, with my direction and future still unknown to me.

"His name is Cole. Has he been here? He just started this route." Lorelei stopped and took a breath, finally giving me enough time to respond.

"I've met him! Yeah, he's hot. He helped me last night when I fell outside the shop and hurt my ankle."

"He's single. I just asked outright. He told me he hasn't met the right girl yet." Lorelei adjusted one of her dangling beaded earrings. "I wonder what Miss Right looks like to him."

I wondered if Miss Right looked like me.

After Lorelei left, I opened the shop, and a steady stream of customers came in to shop or just drink coffee and leaf through the magazines we specifically earmarked for leafing.

A few minutes before 11:00, Sara walked in with Molly, who promptly ran to greet every human in the shop, tail wagging and feathery coat shining in the sunlight that streamed in the window. Kat watched this all unfold from her bed in the front window. If a customer wanted to greet the unusual-looking cat, they had to go to her. Most days she allowed pats, but Sara had put a sign by her bed that people should avoid petting Kat's belly even if it was being offered. It was a trap. A painful trap at that.

"Hey, I'm here. Thanks again for opening today." Sara shrugged off her coat and headed to the kitchenette.

"No worries. I haven't gotten to unpack the carton of new incense yet; it's been pretty busy. Do you want me to do that while you take the register?"

"Sure." Sara poured herself a large mug of coffee. "How are you feeling? About the Cole-Tristan thing? Have you thought more about telling Tristan?"

"I feel like I need to tell him the truth. It's not like I want to break up over this, but I feel this crazy butterfly-stomach-queasy-lightheaded-am-I-getting-the-flu feeling every time I see Cole."

Sara nodded as she sipped her black coffee. "I get it. Well, not the flu feeling, but butterflies? Definitely. When are you supposed to see Tristan again?"

She walked out of the kitchenette and sat on the stool behind the register, waiting for my answer.

"Not for another week, at least. He's got exams to study for."

"Are you planning on telling him in person or on the phone?"

I chewed my lip. "I want to do it by text, but I guess that's wrong. That's chicken, right? He deserves better, right? I should wait for in person."

"Is that partially because that's at least a week away?"

"Yeah." I hung my head. Why was this so complicated? A few days ago, my biggest worry was what to wear to Dad and Sara's upcoming wedding. My feelings for Tristan were all over the place. I loved Tristan. He was my first actual boyfriend, and we had a few magical summers at the beach in Lavallette. He was kind and gentle and never pushed me to do anything I didn't want to do. The growing distance between us directly resulted from the literal distance between us. I wanted something exciting. I wanted something sexy. Something that curled my toes. I wanted what Sara had with my dad. Of course, the moment that thought ran through my mind, I had to swallow back a laugh, because as much as I loved Sara, I couldn't resist teasing them both about being Hallmark movie gooey. But that's what I wanted. I wanted to be starry-eyed and gooey in all the best ways.

I met Sara's eyes and, as always, they held nothing but compassion and love.

"Take a breath… Sleep on it another night and see if you feel the same. If you do, then wait to see him. If you decide not to say anything at all, I'll support you in that as well. Maybe it's just the stress of the holidays combined with the meet-cute you had with Cole that sparked the electricity."

"Maybe." But in my heart, I knew it was not that simple. I had a feeling nothing about this was going to be simple.

CHAPTER 8

SARA

I kept half an eye on Dani for the next few hours. She was a bit withdrawn but perked right up when Cole walked through the door juggling our boxes.

"Hey Dani. Hey Sara. Got a few here for you guys." Cole may have mentioned us both, but his eyes were on Dani the entire time.

He put the boxes near the register, and I watched Dani's face get pinker as she eyed our new delivery guy. By the time he was standing upright, her cheeks were so flushed and her eyes so bright, she looked like she had a fever.

There was so much energy flowing between them you could almost see it. No one could miss the attraction. I had a feeling Tristan was going to be an ex in short order, and that made me sad. We'd grown to be close friends with Lisa and Rachel, Tristan's mom and stepmom. The breakup could affect that friendship, but I hoped it was strong enough to withstand the blow.

Molly ambled over to inspect Cole. She sniffed his work boots and his pant legs and finally nosed his crotch as a show of friendship.

Cole burst out laughing at Molly's antics and ruffled her ears. "You're gorgeous! What's her name?"

Dani jumped in before I could answer.

"That's Molly. She definitely approves of you. Unlike our resident cat, who thinks you're a serial killer or the devil or something."

As if on cue, a long, low growl came from the front window of the shop, scaring the older woman reading nearby. Kat slowly stood, stretched, and stalked into the back room to inspect her food dish. Which looked the same as it did a few minutes ago when she last checked it. Undaunted, she turned around and exited through the curtain separating the breakroom storage area from the shop. As she passed by Cole, not only did she hiss, but her tail also grew three sizes, and I wouldn't have been surprised if fireworks started flying out of the shock of white hair on the top of her head.

Molly, thinking Kat was ready to play, pounced in front of her and danced back and forth, waiting for the cat to engage. Of course, Kat didn't engage. She simply stalked back to her bed, her animosity towards Cole apparently forgotten. It was nap time after all.

After Cole left, Dani started sorting boxes, opening and organizing. I made my way over to a familiar face looking at the newly unpacked incense and asked if I could help her find anything.

"Oh, Sara!" exclaimed Verity Miller, the owner of the familiar face. Verity was a regular, always interested in whatever witchy stuff we might have gotten in since her last visit. "You startled me!"

"I'm so sorry, Verity! I didn't mean to be so quiet." I smiled. "We just unpacked this new incense, and more crystals are coming in later this week."

"It smells good through the box. I think I'll try some. I'm still shopping though, and I would love some coffee if the pot were going?"

"I'll get you a cup. A little sugar, right?"

Verity's love for coffee rivaled mine, except she sweetened hers. I like mine black. Every time someone asked me how I take my coffee, I always said "black like my heart," which made me chuckle, but depending on who's with me, I got either eye rolls or groans. It goes over about as well as my favorite dental joke, which I used as often as I could in my years as a dental office manager. Luckily, it happened often that a 2:30 appointment was available, and I could tell people it's the dentist's favorite time of day. You know, "tooth-hurty"? Dental humor.

I made Verity a coffee and topped mine off at the same time. While she sat in one of the comfortable chairs and sipped her favorite beverage, I walked over to Dani at the register.

"It's been busy. Do you need a break?" I asked her.

"I'm good. One of those boxes was for you, not the bookstore. It's from that cool boho shop in New Hope. Is that your dress, finally?"

"I sure hope so. Nothing like cutting it close."

Our wedding is scheduled for New Year's Day, which is less than a month away, and the dress I'd bought needed altering. I thought I had plenty of time, but nope. The alterations were taking longer than expected. I was trying not to stress, but thinking about dress shopping right before Christmas made my legs shaky.

The box was waiting for me on the table in the breakroom. I grabbed scissors, careful to only cut through tape, and lifted the dress out of the surrounding tissue paper. I heard a gasp behind me.

"It's awesome! I love it! Put it on!"

Dani was clapping her hands, and I knew that if her ankle was feeling better, she would jump up and down.

It was a beautiful dress. It was supposed to be mid-calf-length, but since I'm only a little over five feet tall, it fell to my ankles. I didn't bother having it hemmed; the dress had a handkerchief hem. It was all different layers and lengths, each one coming to a point. Trying to alter that would have been a bear. I loved the colors. It was tie-dyed in blues, greens, and purples. Long sleeves, low-cut, and fitted. All this gym work was paying off big time. It looked like a Morticia dress, only with an explosion of color.

"Go try it on!" Dani exclaimed again, impatient to see the finished look.

I ducked into our little bathroom and stripped off my leggings and sweatshirt. Grateful I had unintentionally chosen the right bra this morning, I placed the dress over my head and let it fall. It only fell to my boobs because, well, they were prominent. Tugging it down, I finally got the dress to settle around my hips and legs. Something wasn't right. There was a full-length mirror attached to the back of the door, so I spun around to see what was wrong. Backwards. Backwards was wrong, so I wriggled it around and found the arms. By now I was sweating with all this exertion in a small space. Satisfied, finally, I looked in the mirror and at once started crying. It was so beautiful, and it somehow captured exactly what I was trying to say. Confidence (which I don't always feel), creativity, and color, with a little chaos thrown in. It fit perfectly.

"Sara! Don't come out, Dad's here," Dani called through the door. "He can't see the dress until the wedding."

"I'm melting in here, and I don't want to sweat all over this dress. Tell Dad to stay away. Better yet, send him out to the register. I'll open the door just for you and then change back."

I heard Dani relay the message and Erik's laughter in return.

"Okay, it's safe. Open up!" Dani sounded as excited as I felt.

I opened the bathroom door, and Dani gasped. Then she began to cry.

"It's perfect. I love it! What shoes are you going to wear?"

"Thank you! I'm not sure." I bit my lip. "I was thinking about my aqua combat boots. But maybe we should make time to go to a shoe store or two. I don't know that they will match as well as I thought they would."

"Agreed." Dani nodded. "You look like you're sweating. Go get changed."

"It's a hot flash." I pulled a little battery-operated fan from my sweatshirt and aimed it to blow directly on my face. Some days were worse than others, and the warmth of the bathroom, combined with a ton of wiggling around, didn't help. I felt a drop slide down my forehead and into my left eye. Which, of course, started burning.

Dani handed me a tissue and stifled a laugh.

"Keep laughing, little girl. You'll understand one day." I patted my forehead with the tissue and held it near my left tear duct. "Stand back. I need to shed this dress right now or I'm going to ruin it."

I peeled the dress down from top to bottom and stepped out of the pool of color at my feet. The fan wasn't powerful enough to keep up with the liquid pouring out of my skin. That wasn't the only downside of the fan. When it's folded up, it looks like a vibrator. And it's pink. I get a lot of raised eyebrows when I whip it out of my pocketbook, and I feel bad sometimes disappointing them.

I was exceedingly glad that I'd worn a tank top under my sweatshirt. I was at least ten minutes away from being able to wear the heavier garment.

I overheard a woman's giggle and Erik's smooth deep voice in response. He regularly attracted a crowd of women around him, which bothered Dani to no end. It didn't bother me. I'm not sure why she felt so strongly about it. She had asked me about that shortly after opening Charms & Chapters.

"Aren't you afraid he'll cheat? Those women fall all over him. Like Drea did." Dani sniffed her displeasure at our former neighbor. "Why doesn't it bother you?"

"Remember how I handled the Drea mess? I realized your father hadn't given me any reason to be suspicious, and my reaction was all mine. He's a chick magnet." I smiled at Dani's gagging motion. "He's a total package, and we are both so grateful to have found each other at this stage of life. I'm not worried."

Dani nodded, but I could see she didn't accept things as easily as I did. Hopefully, that would come with age.

I hung my wedding dress and found a small piece of material to snip, which I planned to carry in my wallet to match the colors. I wrapped the dress up and gently placed it back in its box.

Erik poked his head through the curtain to the breakroom. "Hey beautiful. I just came down to pick up a few things at the market and stopped in for a kiss. How did the dress look and fit?"

"Better than I could have hoped for. Now the only issue is footwear. And choosing how to do my hair."

My hair was long and shot through with white streaks that appeared after we survived the storm in Lavallette. When I was working, it was usually up in a bun, or in a French braid when Dani got the urge to play with it.

"I vote down and we'll make it wavy with my curling iron," Dani said, popping up behind her dad. "That's a hippie dress, and it needs hippie hair."

I couldn't argue with that.

CHAPTER 9

DANI

After my dad retrieved his kiss from Sara, he left to continue with the house decorations. The house seemed to be made for Christmas. The wraparound porch was huge, and it's my favorite sitting spot in the warm weather. Hidden from view behind the ornate railing, I could sit and watch the people, the cars, and my favorite, the large trucks trying to cross the small bridge into Pennsylvania. They're inevitably turned around by authorities after the truckers' GPS fails to warn them it's not passable. It can turn into a real cluster as cars must wait to cross the river while the truck tries to maneuver a U-turn around our tight streets.

"Hey, Dani?" Sara's voice broke through my truck thoughts. "If you want to head home, I can close. You haven't had an early afternoon in over a week. It's not busy. Even Verity left." Verity usually came in and stayed for hours. Sara assumed she was lonely and wanted the company of other humans. She was a sweet, gentle lady and never got in the way, so we let her stay as long as she wanted. There were many days in the summer we had to usher her out while we locked up. But in the colder months, she always left while it was still light.

I wanted to go home early, but what if Cole came in again? I wouldn't want to miss his delivery.

"I don't think Cole is coming back in again today. Everything I was expecting has already arrived." As usual, Sara read my thoughts.

"I love when this happens, but it still creeps me out. That's exactly what I was just thinking."

Sara just smiled and winked at me.

She didn't have to tell me twice. I grabbed my coat and headed outside. As I walked past the gallery, Lorelei spotted me and waved me in.

"Hey girl. I'm having a Christmas party this Saturday night and I want you to come. Bring that cute boyfriend of yours."

My stomach dropped a bit at the "cute boyfriend" part.

"I'm going to have it upstairs," she continued. "It's big enough to hold everyone. I'm inviting a lot of the other shop owners, too. And Cole."

My stomach dropped even more than it had a moment before.

"You don't have to bring anything unless you drink something unusual. I'll have all the basics."

I hoped my face didn't show my emotions about drinking, which were mixed. I wasn't legal yet, and I didn't have a ton of experience with alcohol. My dad had joined Alcoholics Anonymous when mom was pregnant with me, and I had spent more time around recovering drinkers than active ones growing up. Tristan would usually bring a six-pack of beer to share when he came for a visit, but I didn't like the taste. The result was pleasant though, and I could understand how tempting wanting more could be.

I nodded my understanding and Lorelei said she would let me know the time later in the week. I thanked her for the invite and asked if she was planning on inviting Sara.

"No, she's cool and everything, but it's going to be mostly young people." Lorelei's phone rang, and she waved goodbye and scurried behind the counter to answer.

~

When I got home, my dad stood on the porch roof stringing the Christmas lights. Our neighbor Lucas was standing on the ground below him, supervising.

I called hellos to them both and went inside. Tank came waddling out of the kitchen to greet me with a slobbery kiss. Tank was never far from his food bowl—or yours. He looked disappointed I didn't have Molly with me. Of course, bulldogs always look disappointed.

I made myself a cup of tea and walked through the house, admiring what Sara had gotten decorated since they'd been home from the trip. The tree was up and lit, but no ornaments yet. Garland decorated the mantle and the archway leading to the stairs. Sara would eventually fill all that in with ornaments, lights, and poinsettias. This year the tree and the garland were fake; Dad didn't want to take a chance that they would drop all their needles before the wedding. They were planning on holding the wedding in the living room. Since the guest list was tiny, there would be plenty of space once we moved the larger furniture into the garage.

Sara and Dad were keeping the attendees to a bare minimum. Tristan's mom and stepmom were invited, along with Tristan, so that could get awkward. I felt a pit of shame in my stomach again, and I shook my head to clear it. Sara's best friends, Lisa from Michigan and Barb from Texas, a.k.a. her "Cell," were flying in on New Year's Eve and staying at our place. Lisa, (not Tristan's mom, Lisa) was going to officiate, having gone online for her certification just for the wedding. Barb was the wedding coordinator, and her decoration choices were being shipped directly to us. Our neighbor Lucas, his wife Emily, and Dad's sponsor Logan, were the only other invitees. And of course Sara's brother Ethan. They were close, and she was heartbroken when his job took him to Australia. Sara wasn't sure Ethan would make it here from so far away for the wedding, but we all hoped he would for her sake. Ethan had gotten sober a few years before Sara came into our lives, and her having been through that made a big difference when she and my dad got together.

So yeah, not an enormous crowd. We were still a few weeks away from the wedding and I knew my world would be different by then. I feel like my world changes often, so I wasn't too concerned. Except for the whole Tristan thing. That part sucked. He was a good guy. And I loved him, but I didn't know if I was in love with him. Cole made me feel a certain way that bordered on dangerous and incredibly sexy at the same time. Like I've just met the bad boy mothers warn their daughters about.

Thinking about Cole took my mind off Tristan, and I stood in front of my closet, deciding on tomorrow's outfit. I had noticed that today's combination didn't seem to catch Cole's eye as much as I'd expected.

I checked my phone for tomorrow's weather report. Sunny, 35 degrees. The bit of snow and ice that caused me to hurt my ankle were already gone. Flipping through the hangers, I chose a sweater dress in gorgeous shades of green and paired it with black leggings. A pair of black suede slouch boots would be perfect. Unfortunately, my favorite pair lives in Sara's closet. I texted her to make sure I could borrow them in the morning.

Tomorrow's outfit complete, I turned my attention to Lorelei's party this weekend. Cole might be there. I might talk to him for longer than just the few minutes we've had since my fall. I chewed my lip as I slid the hangers from one side of the closet to the other. Nothing stood out as a brilliant choice, and I felt a touch of anxiety. I chewed harder. Lorelei would be dressed to kill. Her wardrobe was even quirkier than Sara's. They both could get away with clothes that would make me look ridiculous. Maybe there was something in Sara's closet I could borrow. We shared clothes every so often, but whereas Sara was short and curvy, I'm taller and less curvy in all departments. We couldn't share everything, but now and again, something would work. Thankfully, shoes always fit because we wore the same size.

Visions of Cole danced in my head, and I fantasized about finding him in my stocking Christmas morning.

Cole in my stocking. Why did that sound so ominous?

CHAPTER 10

SARA

I puttered around the shop after Dani left. The last customer checked out, and I was straightening a shelf of books when Kat stretched and jumped from her windowsill bed. I followed her into the back room, where she leaped onto the small table. Before I could shoo her off, she batted the satin bag holding my favorite tarot deck with her paw and pushed it to the ground. She met my eyes, hers questioning. Mine probably looked shocked that this funny-looking cat just deliberately did that. I squatted down to pick the bag up and placed it back on the table where it belonged.

Kat rolled her eyes at me. Now I was no cat expert, but I was sure they couldn't roll their eyes. She once again pushed the satin bag with her paw and dropped it over the side of the table, never taking her green eyes off mine.

"What? Are you trying to tell me something?"

Kat cocked her head to the side and let out a small meow.

I bent over once again and picked up the satin bag.

"Fine. Let's do this."

Before taking the tarot cards out of the bag, I checked the shop, making sure a customer hadn't come in while I was busy in the back room. Molly was asleep on her bed and all was quiet. It was almost closing time anyway, so I reached up to pull the shade on the front door. As my hand was about to curl around the drawstring, there was a knock.

I jumped back, gasping.

"I'm so sorry, Sara!" exclaimed Cole, opening the door. "I thought you saw me. I found a package for you on the truck. Glad I caught you before you closed."

A low growl came from the back room and Molly came over to say hello with her nose to Cole's crotch.

"No worries! I was just closing a little early since the shop was empty."

"Is Dani still here?" he asked, patting Molly and looking around the shop.

Another hiss and spit at the sound of his voice.

"No, I sent her home a couple of hours ago."

Cole looked disappointed. I could see why Dani was so drawn to him. He was strikingly handsome, his muscles clearly defined through his well-fitting uniform, and he had great lips. Hey, I love my husband-to-be beyond measure, but I can still appreciate a good-looking young guy!

"Do you know if she's going to Lorelei's party Saturday night?" he asked.

I paused before answering, expecting another reaction from Kat, and was rewarded with a combo of hiss, spit, and moan.

"I didn't know there was a party. I have heard nothing about it."

"I thought Lorelei said she was inviting the local store owners, but maybe I was wrong. I'll ask Dani tomorrow." With a wave, Cole closed the door behind him, and I pulled the shade and locked it again.

Kat came through the curtain into the shop and glared at me, her green eyes flashing sparks. She turned and stalked back through the curtain, expecting me to follow. I tend to be a rule follower, so that's what I did.

I sat at the little table after pouring the last of the coffee from the pot into my mug. Molly joined us and curled up at my feet. Kat jumped up on the other chair and looked at me expectantly.

I pulled the drawstring open and removed the cards, which were wrapped in one of my colorful silk scarves. I slowly shuffled and thought about my intentions. The card pull was Kat's idea, so I wasn't quite sure where to focus. I thought about everything on my mind. My wedding would be here before I knew it, but luckily Barb's role as wedding planner took a huge amount of work off my plate. The shop practically ran itself; it was popular, and I had no worries about that nagging at my brain. Erik brought me joy daily, same with our home and animals. Dani and I have a close relationship, and we get along well, and I decided my worries revolved around her more than anyone or anything else. The possible breakup with Tristan, the electricity flowing between her and Cole, and Dani's own indecision about her future were more than enough to set an intention. I quickly realized I wanted to read for Dani, not myself, and sent her a text asking if she'd mind.

Permission granted. Shuffle, cut, pull. And the big winner was one of the Major Arcana cards, the Lovers Reversed. I let out a sigh and reached for my book. I'm still a beginner and just learning the patterns of the deck and the card meanings. Since I only read for myself or family, I enjoy having the book to reinforce what I'm interpreting.

It's possible you are struggling and uncertain about the direction your life is going in. You may be feeling conflict about decisions which need to be made. Learn lessons, let go, and move forward.

Kat made a mewling sound and pushed the card around until it was upright. I turned back a page in the book, to the Lovers card, to satisfy my curiosity. Apparently this cat has some magic in her.

There is a choice to be made. Lovers should listen to their hearts. There is vice and virtue awaiting your choice.

I had to chuckle at the power of intention. The Universe proves it to me again and again.

CHAPTER 11

DANI

I was in the kitchen feeding Tank when Molly and Sara came in the side door. I poured kibble in Molly's bowl as well. No doubt she was famished from sleeping in her bed all day.

"Hey!" I called out to Sara.

"Hey yourself! Wait until I tell you how the reading went. You will not believe it." Sara hung her coat on a hook and kicked off her boots. "And I always knew there was something special about Kat, but tonight I saw all kinds of weird stuff."

My dad came into the kitchen in time to hear the end of her sentence.

"You saw weird stuff tonight?" he asked. "Do I need to chaperone you 24/7 to make sure you stay out of mischief?"

Sara laughed and stood on her tiptoes to give him a kiss. Molly broke away from her dinner to rush at my dad, something she's done since the first time she met him. Some things never change. They ended up in a three-way hug before Molly decided dinner was once again her priority. Sara laughed and shooed Dad out of the kitchen.

"I need to talk girl stuff with Dani. Would you be a love and carry that laundry basket upstairs to our bedroom?"

My father went off on his mission. Sara and I sat at the table so she could fill me in. She grabbed my hands, and I noticed hers were vibrating slightly.

"Sara, how much coffee did you have today?"

"Well, when Verity asked for a cup this afternoon, I refreshed my mug and then before I pulled your card, I finished the pot. Why? Am I vibrating?"

"Yeah." I laughed. "Your lower lip is too."

"Some of that is the magic that happened earlier," Sara replied. She explained what went on with Kat. "Oh! I forgot! Cole came back. He brought a package that was missed during his earlier delivery. Which reminds me, I put it behind the register and forgot to open it. Dammit."

"Do you want me to run back there and get it?" I asked.

"No, no need. I'll open Charms in the morning and get it then. I never even looked at who it was from."

"Okay, so tell me about the reading."

Sara had written everything down that she interpreted earlier. She passed it to me, and I had to laugh.

"Wow. Talk about nailing it."

"Right? And Kat. She was more human than a cat. You should have heard the sounds coming out of her when Cole was there."

"Yeah, Kat hates him. I've never seen her react to anyone like that in all the time we've had her at the shop. I mean, she'll ignore people all day long but to hiss and spit, that's totally out of character."

Sara gave me a searching look. "Between that, the reading, and your flu-like feeling, sounds like you have a lot of crap to think about."

She spoke the truth. Sara always spoke the truth. But she had a way of saying things with love, so it never sounded bossy or judgmental. I always knew where I stood in her life. She treated me like the daughter she never had and taught me daily how to be a better human.

I dropped my head into my hands. "Why does life have to be so freaking complicated?"

"Life can be complicated. But if you address each layer, one at a time, you'll get through everything on your plate. Eventually. And just in time for more crap to collect on your plate. It's just how it can be. You can get through whatever is thrown your way. You haven't croaked yet, right?"

I laughed. "Not yet. But a zombie apocalypse is always on the horizon."

After confirming with Sara that I could borrow her black suede boots in the morning, I opened my laptop and scrolled through my social media. I did a few more disappointing searches for Cole and shut the laptop again. Fruitless until I find out his last name.

My stomach started growling, so I texted Sara.

DANI
Dinner?

The three dots jumped.

SARA
How does Thai takeout sound?

DANI
Amazing. You know my order.

I wiggled with anticipation, knowing soon I'd be enjoying #28 with great delight. And it took my mind off the chaos in my life.

My dad ran down the street to pick up our order while Sara and I set the table.

"Oh! I forgot something else. Cole asked me if you were going to Lorelei's party on Saturday night. I didn't know she was having one. He mentioned a few shop owners were invited."

"It's just for a few younger people. That's okay, right? You're not upset?"

"But I'm like twenty-three in my brain." Sara was pushing sixty, although she didn't look it.

I laughed. "I know. But you get it, right? It's in her apartment above the gallery, so I'll be close to home."

"Of course I do. Have fun. Be careful. What are you going to wear?"

"I have no clue. Can I look in your closet? Maybe a skirt and one of my tops. Shoes or boots. I don't know. Lorelei's going to be so flashy, it probably won't matter what I wear."

"She has an amazing look. I wish I'd had the guts to wear stuff like that when I was her age. My no-fucks era didn't begin until my fifties."

"You both always look perfect." I sighed.

"Dani, you do too! Just be comfortable. Wearing uncomfortable clothing just drains the life out of your day. Soft stretchy fabrics are my rule. They never let me down," Sara said. "Except for that one time at physical therapy when I didn't realize my leggings were see-through. That butterfly pose must have given all the other people quite a show."

I snorted. Sara was a self-admitted awkward girl and extremely clumsy, so I didn't doubt she put everything on display for the other PT patients and therapists.

Tank waddled to the kitchen door and woofed, which meant food was on its way in and girl talk had ended. I gave Sara a quick hug.

"Thanks for letting me raid your closet. And thanks for the

advice. I'll start working on the layers on my plate as soon as I work on the layers on my dinner plate."

That got a groan and an eye roll from Sara, so I guess my work there was done.

CHAPTER 12

SARA

My eyes opened at the ungodly hour of 4:30 a.m., and as much as I tried to fall back asleep, nothing worked. I swear once I'm awake, I'm awake. Erik was snoring softly on my right. Molly was curled at my feet, snoring louder than Erik. I slipped out of bed and hit the bathroom before wrapping my big fuzzy purple robe around me. I tried to be as quiet as possible going downstairs, but it's an old house and there were no safe spots to step that wouldn't creak. It was loud enough to wake Tank up, and he met me at the bottom of the stairs wiggling his tail-less butt as a good morning greeting.

I let him out into our fenced yard and added water to the kettle for tea. When I'm up this early, I start my day with tea instead of coffee. That black magic comes after the tea is consumed and the morning is welcomed.

Scratching at the back door reminded me that Tank was outside, and he came in grumbling, probably about the temperature. I wouldn't want to leave my warm bed to go pee outside in 25-degree weather either. I'm extremely grateful I was born, at least in this lifetime, after indoor plumbing had been invented.

I plugged in the Christmas lights and curled up in Erik's recliner with my Earl Grey, the smell of bergamot rising with the steam. My plan after work included putting ornaments on the tree and working on the garland draped along the archway between the living room and the foyer. I wasn't usually a big fan of fake greenery, including trees, but I had to admit everything Erik picked out looked so close to real you expected needles to fall. We still had a couple of weeks before the wedding, but the tree looked so bare. I made a mental note to have Erik bring down all the boxes of decorations from the attic. There was no way I was climbing up or down the death stairs.

The first thing I did after opening the shop was grab the small box from behind the counter. It was beat up and dirty. The shipping label obscured most of the handwriting underneath, but I could see my name written in tiny script peeking out from behind it. No return address, just a single name above a PO box.

Lily.

Chills ran throughout my body. I never saw Lily again after our magical encounter. I had walked past her property daily with Molly, but she was never visible (or audible, given that I had heard her before I ever saw her). After my second summer in Lavallette, her unique gardens looked neglected rather than beautifully chaotic. The vines overtook the statues instead of being lovingly trimmed back. I searched the internet but since I had little to go on, nothing came up for her. I checked the tax records for the property and found listed a large real estate corporation.

I held the package gently while I wondered how she found me. Then I smiled because Lily was clearly capable of all sorts of magic.

I slid a scissor under the tape holding the small box together. Opening the flaps revealed tissue paper wrapped around a very well-used tarot deck. The chills up and down my back came again as I held the deck in my hands. There was a small envelope with my name on it, in the same handwriting as the return address.

My hands shook slightly as I opened the envelope and read Lily's words.

Sara,

My apologies for not being in contact sooner. I am sending you the deck I used for your reading. My mother passed it along to me many decades ago. We've handed it down through generations of females in my family. The bloodline stops with me though, which makes me so sad, and for so long, I wondered what I would do with it when my time here was done.

And then I met you.

My darling girl, I saw your gift when you entered my gardens that day. Wouldn't it have been lovely to discover we were long-lost relatives?

I am sure you should be the new owner of this deck. Add your magic through each use, and make sure, when it's your time to pass it along, you give it to the right person. Just like I did.

The story of why you never saw me again is so long, and my time is short. So, I beg your forgiveness, and pray we meet again on another plane...

Take good care of the deck, Sara... it holds many answers if you know where to look.

Blessed be.

Lily

Tears streamed down my face as I read and reread Lily's note. Then I noticed the date on the label. It was the same month we opened Charms & Chapters. The package had taken that long to get to me? I made a mental note to ask Cole where he found it. From the look of the worn and tattered box, my guess was that it got stuck somewhere, behind something, accidentally shoved in a corner and overlooked.

I checked the date on the label again and compared it to the calendar on my phone to see what was going on in my life around that time. A strange idea was growing that I almost didn't want to entertain but couldn't stop thinking about.

The week after Lily mailed the package, we were doing the final walk-through of the shop before signing all the papers. And that was the day Kat walked into our lives with her strange, long sprout of stark white hair.

I dropped the box on the counter. The chills were running from my scalp to my toes now. Lily? Kat? WTF? But how did Lily have the address for Charms & Chapters if we hadn't signed the lease yet?

I texted Dani.

SARA

Hey. How soon are you coming in?

I have something strange to talk to you about.

Her answer came back right away.

DANI

OMW shortly

She was going to think I was having some type of breakdown, or she might actually believe me. I wasn't sure which way that was going to go. If she didn't believe me, I would just put this out of my head and laugh off that I'd even consider something so ludicrous.

And if she believed me, then what on earth would our next step be? Go find Kat and confront her? Ask the cat directly if she was Lily reincarnated?

I laughed out loud at myself for even thinking that.

I stopped laughing when Kat appeared out of nowhere, jumped on the counter, and stared at me. I stared back, and goosebumps erupted again.

"Lily?" I whispered.

CHAPTER 13

DANI

When I got Sara's text, I stopped puttering around my room and got dressed. The outfit I chose looked spectacular, if I did say so myself. Sara's boots were the perfect addition. If Cole didn't notice this one, I might just go to the party naked. I felt my face flush as the thought of Cole seeing me nude raced through my brain. Then the flu-like feeling hit, the punch of shame I got when I was reminded that Tristan exists.

I ran downstairs, grabbed my coat, and kissed my dad on the top of his head as he sat at the kitchen table drinking coffee and working on a crossword puzzle.

"Are you going in already? I thought Sara was taking the early shift."

"I am. She just texted me she had a strange story to tell me, so I don't want to wait any longer. I love her stories."

Dad looked up from his puzzle. "She definitely has some unusual stories. Things just seem to happen to her. I don't know if she attracts strange or strange attracts her."

Honestly? Could go either way.

~

Sara looked up from her perch at the counter as I entered Charms & Chapters. "Oh, thank goodness. I need a rational person to tell me whether what I think is happening is or is not actually happening."

I shut the door behind me, raised the shade, and flipped the sign to Open since it was actually a few minutes past time.

"I got here as soon as I could. Tell me what happened!"

Sara took a deep breath. "Look at the box that Cole delivered last night. Real beat up and dirty, right? Look at the postmark date on the label. It's old. It was mailed here, to Charms & Chapters, one week before we signed the papers. So that's one mystery."

"I might be able to solve that one. We were doing a lot of social media in the months before we found the exact right storefront, and more after we found it. Plus, a couple of weeks passed after our first visit before we signed the papers. A simple search would have brought up your name and then the posts about Charms & Chapters."

Sara seemed to be thinking about that, as if the timeline were playing out in her head. "Okay, I can see that happening. Good thinking."

"Go on, go on. I'm waiting for strange."

"The package is from Lily."

Now it was getting more interesting. I knew Sara always wanted to contact Lily again. "Wow! After all this time, you finally heard from her. What did she say?"

"Here's the note. I want you to read it for yourself. The box held this deck of tarot cards. It was the deck she used when she did my reading that day."

Sara handed me the letter, and I read it quickly. Tears sprang to my eyes when I realized that it meant Lily had passed away.

"I'm so sorry, Sara. I know you felt a special connection with her. It's so cool though, that she saw how magical you are. But I wouldn't say it's strange. What haven't you told me?"

Sara looked over at Kat, asleep on her bed in the window. "Kat showed up out of the blue on the day we signed the papers. With that strange hair. That strange long white tuft of hair or fur or whatever you would call that."

I sat with all that for a bit. "Sara, are you saying what I think you're saying?"

"Yes. I'm saying it. I'm saying I think Kat is Lily somehow. Whether it's reincarnation or a spell or some type of magic, I don't know. But yes. I'm saying it." Sara looked at me for my reaction before continuing. "You think that's just ridiculous, right? You're going to tell me I'm not thinking clearly and I'm just projecting my sadness at losing Lily into a fantasy."

I thought about all of this. The timing made sense. But that's about the only thing that did. "I don't know. I'm not so sure about it."

Sara's face fell, then looked relieved. "Okay. That's what I needed to hear. I'm going to forget I even thought the thought."

With that said, Sara slid off the stool and went to go start a pot of her beloved coffee.

I looked over at Kat while Sara's words kept playing in my mind. As if she knew I was staring at her, Kat opened her eyes and lifted her head. She met my gaze and stretched one front leg out, spreading her toe beans, then pulled it back to clean her face.

Ridiculous, I thought. Utter nonsense. Sara had some weird shit happen to her and around her, but this was off the charts, even for Sara.

Kat paused her cleaning routine and looked at me again. I mean, this cat was strange, there was no denying that. And she'd gotten even stranger since Cole came into our lives.

Sara came out of the back room with her favorite mug full of steaming black coffee and a smaller mug with a little milk added for me. I just can't drink it black like she does.

"Thanks," I said gratefully.

"You're welcome. Great outfit, by the way. The boots go perfectly. You look amazing."

I struck a pose. Sara laughed. So I struck another pose and kept changing position, looking a little like I was swatting flies. Of course, that's when Cole walked by the front window, caught sight of me, and started laughing. He poked his head in the front door just to bust my ass. I knew I was blushing at his reaction but started laughing when I saw how hard Sara was trying not to laugh.

"Okay, okay. I'm so glad I could brighten both your days," I said with mock indignation. "Laugh. I don't even care."

Sara couldn't hold it in any longer and laughed until tears ran down her cheeks. Cole was still chuckling, but I saw him check out my outfit with appreciative eyes.

Relief washed over me when I realized that meant I didn't have to go to Lorelei's party naked.

Small victories.

CHAPTER 14

SARA

Once the three of us stopped laughing and collected ourselves, I waved Cole in and questioned him about the package from Lily.

"I don't know, Sara. Sorry. Found it stuffed behind a bench in the truck. I never saw it on my delivery manifest and that label looks old. Did you ask the person who sent it?"

I got a lump in my throat. "No, I can't ask her. I think she's passed away."

"Sorry again, Sara. I wish I could help more. I could ask someone for you. Let me see the label. I'll take a picture."

Last night's reading put me on edge with Cole.

"No, thanks, it's okay. It really doesn't matter. It made it here, and that's the important thing."

Kat was just coming out of the back room and hissed when she saw Cole. The hair along her spine stood straight up in the air and her tail puffed up to twice its normal size.

"Kat! Be nice," Dani said as she scooped the cat into her arms, hoping to avoid bloodshed.

A low growl erupted from Kat's throat, and her eyes flashed lightning bolts at Cole.

"I don't think I'm ever going to win her over," Cole said with a rueful smile. "I just want to be friends."

An even lower growl came out of Kat, and Cole backed away with his hands up. He was about to open the door when Verity burst through it, almost knocking him over. She didn't even acknowledge him.

"Sara! You must smell this. It's terrible," Verity said breathlessly. "I mean, it smells like…" She paused and whispered, "The men's room at the bar down the street."

I thought about whether I wanted to know how she knew that.

Verity held the box of incense she'd bought the day before. She practically threw it towards me like it was on fire. I must have looked skeptical.

"Go on. Light one up. You'll see."

I held the box to my nose, and while I couldn't quite place the smell, it wasn't as bad as a public men's room. I pulled out a stick and brought it to the back room. Grabbing a lighter, I slid the stick into a leather incense holder and lit it.

I didn't have to wait long for the smell of a urinal cake to hit me. That is one of those smells you never forget. It instantly brought back memories of clubbing in the '80s and having to use the men's room because the line for the ladies' room was so long, you'd pee yourself waiting. This is one reason women always go to the bathroom in packs. Someone to stand guard, find toilet paper, run the water in the sink, hold the stall door closed for you, lend a tampon. It's just something we do.

I dunked the lit stick into some water in the sink, sprayed some air freshener, and went back out into the shop.

"Yup. You are not wrong. That's a urinal cake smell."

Verity puffed up a bit at my praise.

"It's disgusting, right? Can I get my money back? Or store credit or something?"

67

"Of course," I assured her. "Whichever you prefer. You can take a box of one of the tried-and-true brands if you'd like."

That made Verity happy, and she walked over to the incense display to peruse all the scents.

Cole had left when Verity entered, but Dani was still standing by the register. I gave her the lowdown on the new incense.

"I do not know what that smells like. Is that an old people thing? How do *you* know what that smells like?" Dani cocked her head and wiggled her eyebrows. "Why were you in the men's room, Sara?"

"Haven't you ever been in a long ladies' room line?"

"Yeah, but I never used the men's room instead. Ew. Were there guys in there while you were going to the bathroom?"

Dani's face showed she was grossed out and her lips puckered with disapproval.

"Of course not. One of my posse would cover the door and keep them out," I said with a swagger in my voice.

"Your posse? Oh my God. Did you just say *posse?*"

She didn't understand the pack mentality of being in a club. Yet. I knew it was going to happen at some point, but I also knew Erik had talked to her openly about his alcoholism and how that gene can be handed down through generations, so maybe her experiences would be different from mine.

"Someday I'll tell you those stories, little girl."

Dani was laughing out loud now. "Posse stories?"

"Yes. Posse stories. But another day and time. Right now, I need to get that carton of urinal cake incense back to the manufacturer before anyone else gets disgusted by them. I think Verity was the only customer to buy a box."

"I kind of want to smell it," Dani admitted. "Light another one up in the back room. Please?"

I groaned. "Seriously? How about I just take you into the men's room in the bar down the street?"

"I think Dad would disapprove." Dani looked at me, and I could tell she was trying not to laugh.

"Smart ass." I waved my hand towards the curtain. "After you. Remember, you asked for it."

I lit the stick and filled a small cup of water to set next to it for fast extinguishing. The tendrils of smoke drifted past our noses.

"Oh my God," Dani cried out. She grabbed the stick and dunked it into the water. "That is disgusting. No wonder Verity brought it back."

I had to admit; the smell was noxious at best. I knew I was taking a chance on this new brand, but the price was so good I couldn't pass up the deal.

I should have passed up the deal.

CHAPTER 15

DANI

I lit an incense stick I had used before and trusted to cover the odor of what I knew now was a urinal cake. Sara was on the phone with the manufacturer, setting up the return. We primarily stock items from small businesses and try to keep everything as local as possible. The urinal cake incense was produced just a few miles from our shop.

"Annie, I'm sorry, but we need to send back that carton of incense. It just doesn't have a pleasant odor, and we already have a return from a customer." ... "Yes, I tried, we just lit one here and had to put it out right away." ... "A urinal cake." ... "I said *a urinal cake*. Do you know what that smells like?" ... "No? Well, it's not good." ... "That's none of your business." ... "Then light one when you get it back and smell for yourself." ... "I'll have Erik bring the carton back himself. Please credit the card back?" ... "Thank you."

Sara looked a bit stressed as she hung up, so I freshened her coffee and patted her shoulder in solidarity. We both hate phone calls. Making them, answering them, all of it. It can be a struggle when the shop phone rings, so we take turns and keep a tally on a whiteboard behind the counter. Another one hangs in the back room near that phone. That's how much we hate phone calls. When Sara was away, I had to answer and make all the calls, so she owes me.

～

Customers started coming in and Sara was busy behind the counter when Cole entered with a fairly small Special Delivery package.

"Just this so far, but I think I have more for later. It has your home address on it, but I checked here first since it's an air freight package."

He looked scrumptious in his uniform. I took the package from him and focused on his hands. They were as gorgeous as his lips. Manly hands. Rough. Calloused. Red from the cold. I felt myself turning pink as I pictured those hands touching me. Those icy hands cupping my face, hot with need.

"Thanks," I said, coming back to earth. I looked at the return address. A hotel in Abu Dhabi. My mother's name below it. I felt my heart pound. Why would she mail me something and not just text or call?

I ripped it open and pulled out a small flat box wrapped in Christmas paper and a small card, which still held the scent of my mother's expensive perfume.

"My darling Danielle, our cruise has been delayed in Abu Dhabi, and I don't think we'll be home for Christmas. I found your gift in a lovely open market here and sent it, so you'll have something for Christmas morning. I'll be in touch with our new arrival day when I find out. Love, Mom."

I shook the little box to hear if it rattled. Nothing. She'd never know if I opened it now or on Christmas morning, right? Right. I gently lifted the tape on the wrapping, careful not to tear the paper for re-wrapping purposes. The box inside was elegant as hell, with sterling silver corner accents, inlaid pearl sides, and an ornate sterling latch.

"What did you get?" asked Sara once the last customer left. "Ooh, what a beautiful box! Who's it from?"

"My mom. Her cruise ship is delayed in Abu Dhabi, so she won't be home for Christmas."

"Dammit, I'm sorry. Is there anything inside?"

I flipped the latch and lifted the lid. The box was lined in a deep violet satin. In the middle was a tiny bottle of perfume. That explained why the paper held her scent. It was my mother's favorite.

"Perfume." I held it up for Sara to see. "It's pretty." I put it back in the box and closed the latch. "I love this box; I can put my favorite rings in here."

"It is stunning. I'm glad it survived the shipping. So, when is she coming back through?"

"I don't know. According to her note, she wasn't sure but said she would text me. I haven't heard anything yet, and it's been several days since she mailed this, so who knows?" I shrugged. Originally, they were flying into New York on the 23rd and driving here to see me for Christmas. They had a week booked at a local bed and breakfast, flying out to their next adventure on the 30th. It didn't really bother me she wouldn't be here for Christmas. Ever since she married Chris, it was one trip after another. Occasionally, those trips meant she'd be away for a birthday or holiday. Cruises were their favorite thing to do, and they spent a lot of time in glamorous ports around the world.

Sara's face grew concerned.

"I wonder if they'll be here for the wedding." Sara's voice was flat, and I assumed she was afraid my mom would pull a wedding crasher move.

"I don't think she'd come, Sara." I shrugged. "It would be awkward for her, too."

"Yeah, I guess you're right. If the roles were reversed, I wouldn't want to be anywhere near it."

"And remember, they've been divorced a long time, and she's been married to Chris for years. So, there's no reason to be jealous of her."

"No, I know that," Sara continued. "And it's not jealousy. It's fear."

"Fear? Why?"

"I had a dream shortly after your dad proposed. We were at a wedding, and I was in the ladies' room washing my hands." Sara's face fell. "The door opened, your mother walked in with a gun in her hands, and she shot me."

My jaw practically hit the floor.

"I don't remember you ever telling me about that!"

"Never did. It was just a dream, but it seriously stuck with me for a long time. The thought of your mother and me at a wedding together sends a shiver down my spine." Sara looked down at her feet. "Silly, I know. Just a dream."

"Just a dream," I repeated. "Shall we have some coffee while it's quiet in here?"

"Do you even need to ask?"

CHAPTER 16

SARA

My phone dinged as I sat in the back room sipping my coffee. My brother.

Hey Sis,

Sorry about telling you this in an email, but with the time difference, a phone call is just too difficult. Wanted to let you know I won't be alone when I come back for your wedding. Met someone a few months ago, and we just got married. I can't wait for you guys to meet. Her name is Diana. She's amazing. And my stepson Jace will join us as well. He has always wanted to travel to the States, and we figured, why not? He's a good kid, 23. Responsible. We got another room for him at the Belvidere Hotel next to us. Can't wait to see you and meet Erik finally. Hey, I celebrated 8 years last week with Diana by my side and I couldn't be happier. See you in a few weeks.

Love,

Ethan

I read his email over three times. This was big, even for Ethan. He'd been single a long time, and a heavy drinker for much of his adult life. I never thought he'd straighten out, but he did it. And he's thriving. I was thrilled for him. We could squeeze two extra people into the living room on New Year's Day.

∾

It was late afternoon, and I was ready to leave when Erik came in to let me know he returned the carton of urinal cake incense without issue. Apparently, Annie had lit one and immediately realized there was a mistake in the recipe somewhere.

"Thanks, babe. I was just about to leave for the day. My goal is to decorate the tree tonight. Did you get the boxes down for me?"

"I did. Those stairs are dicey. I'm glad this only happens once a year."

"Thanks for not breaking yourself or any ornaments in your journey." I purred and stood on my tiptoes to kiss his gorgeous face.

"You're welcome. Do you want to ride home with me, or walk?"

He knew I liked to get my steps in as often as possible. "Ride. I want to be in touching range."

"Ermergerd!" Dani cried out. "Do you guys ever give it a rest?"

"Sorry, kiddo. No rest." Erik laughed.

Dani put up her hand and dramatically said, "Go. Just go."

I laughed at her theatrics. I've been dramatic since I was a little girl. My mother always called me Sara Heartburn.

"C'mon, big guy. Let's go make out in your car." Since it was a nice day, Erik had taken out his prized possession, a fully restored 1957 turquoise and white, two-door Bel Air convertible with a nice big front seat.

The possibilities were endless. Too bad it was only two blocks and everyone along those two blocks knew who we were.

"You got it, baby. Ready to rock and roll?" Erik did some kind of Elvis move with his hips, which made me snort and made Dani put her face in her hands.

"You guys are such dorks. Seriously. Can you both please just go home and be dorky there?"

"With pleasure." Erik smirked. "Molly and Tank don't care if we're dorky."

I ran my finger across his cheek. "That front seat is waiting, baby. Let's go."

We linked pinkies and danced our way out of the door, much to Dani's horror. Of course, that only made us shimmy even harder down the sidewalk. And laugh. God, I loved this man. This goofy, happy, centered, beautiful man who shows me every day what it means to be unconditionally loved.

He claims I wouldn't have liked him when he was drinking. That he was not a man of honor and grew to hate the man he was. He told me about his booze-filled days and his booze-filled haze. How he thought he was a better writer when he had a few drinks. And he told me how AA was there for him when he finally asked for help, which was why he still stayed active in the program and had an enormous network across the country. Erik liked to immerse himself in whatever surroundings he's writing about, so he's traveled all over, and he sought out a meeting whenever he could. He had established himself with a local group since we moved here, and I still loved going to celebration meetings with him to support members making sobriety milestones. Plus, there's always cake. And coffee. It's not always good coffee, but when you add cake to the picture, it makes everything better.

Erik opened my car door, and I slid into the big front seat. When he has the car out on a warm day, he likes to put the convertible top down and vault into the front seat over the door. I tried to do that once when no one was looking. My legs weren't long enough, so I was thwarted immediately. I'm sure the sight of me trying to get my foot up on the car was worth recording. It took me several tries before I finally gave up. I'm stubborn like that.

My handsome husband-to-be drove us the couple of blocks to our home. How we found this house felt like kismet. I fell in love with the place when we drove by it on our way to view the empty building that we had hoped would hold Charms & Chapters. I remember pointing it out to Erik and Dani. From the outside the pretty gray house checked all the boxes on our dream Victorian wish list. Erik offered to stop on our way back to Lavallette and see if the owners were home and possibly interested in selling. It was wild how I could barely make a trivial phone call without having a panic attack and he could walk up to total strangers and ask if they want to sell their home.

We then looked at the empty retail building and took some notes, photos, and measurements. I remember feeling excited about what we saw, because I could picture how a bookstore might fit perfectly. We shook hands with the landlord and told him we would sleep on it and talk again tomorrow. Erik pointed the car back to the beach. As we drove past that Victorian home, slowly this time, there was an older man pushing a sign into the front yard.

FOR SALE BY OWNER.

Yeah. This was the stuff that kept happening to me, and I wasn't even sure how or why half the time.

Erik pulled over and we got out of the car. We introduced ourselves and told the man how much we loved the house. He introduced himself as Angelo Merrill and invited us to tour the inside, which turned out to be just as spectacular as the outside. The ceilings, the floors, the architecture, and the vibe all worked together to make me want to sign the papers right then and there. Erik checked out all the stuff men are concerned about when buying a house, things I know nothing about, and when he came up from the basement, he gave me a covert thumbs-up.

It took us about ten minutes to agree on a price. We shook on it and before we knew it, it was ours. Erik and I planned on keeping the beach house for special times away, so after a quick closing and some furniture shopping, we moved into our magical home. Within a couple of weeks, we signed the papers on the building where we would open Charms & Chapters.

With a mental shake to clear my head, I turned to Erik as the front door closed behind us. "I'm going to jump right into decorating since you brought the boxes down. Do you want to help?" I asked.

Erik grabbed me around the waist and pulled me into a long, deep kiss.

"Nope. I want you to come upstairs with me. Dani won't be home for a couple of hours, and I plan on making you scream. In a good way, of course."

"You remember it's winter and my legs are in yeti season, right?"

"Like I care about that." He growled in my ear. "Your fur doesn't bother me."

A wave of lust spread through my pelvic floor, and I dashed up the stairs as quickly as my short legs could manage.

"Don't keep me waiting!" I called over my shoulder.

He didn't.

CHAPTER 17

DANI

J ust as I was going to flip our Open sign to Closed, Lorelei
appeared at the door.

"Hey girl. I wanted to drop off the party info and make
sure you were going to come."

"Absolutely! I'm still deciding what I want to wear."

"I can help with that. I want this to be an ugly sweater party.
Contest winner gets a piece of art from me."

"I don't have an ugly Christmas sweater. I don't even have a cute
Christmas sweater."

"Girl, I've got you. I have at least six. Come over when you're
done, and you can choose one."

After closing, I walked up to Lorelei's gallery and noticed the
delivery truck parked in front. My heart started thumping in my
chest and I couldn't swallow. Why does he have this effect on me?
Just seeing his truck made me tingle.

I entered the shop and saw Cole leaning on the counter, smiling
and chatting with Lorelei. A white-hot bolt of jealousy almost
knocked me off my feet, which surprised the hell out of me.

"Dani!" Lorelei called out when she finally looked away from Cole. "We were just talking about Saturday night. Cole promised to bring some fun stuff."

And then she winked at him.

I stretched my mouth into what I hoped was a smile. I'm not really sure, though. At worst, it was a grimace. My brain kept showing me that wink. Over and over in slow motion until my eye twitched.

"Fun stuff?" I asked with a level of brightness I didn't mean. Anything to get Cole's attention away from Lorelei.

"Hey, Dani. I want it to be a surprise for everyone, but I needed to clear it with Lorelei first." Cole put his hand on my shoulder. "How is your ankle feeling?"

Ankle. Oh yeah. My ankle. The ankle we met over. The ankle that made me kiss him. Twice.

"It's fine. A little tender, but if I wear sturdy boots, it seems to be okay." I gave him a smile, a genuine smile, and added, "Thanks for asking."

I glanced at Lorelei to see if she had any reaction to Cole's attention on me. Her face was a neutral mask, but she was watching us closely. Could they be involved already? Or was she just showing an interest in being involved?

"Okay, ladies, I must be getting back to work. I'll probably see you both tomorrow." Cole gave us each a salute and left the gallery.

The door was barely shut when Lorelei squealed, "GAAAAAAAH! He's so hot. I'm surprised there's not a puddle on the floor beneath me."

First—*ew*. Second—more *EW*. That was more information than I needed to know about her. Now I had to shake the memory of the wink *and* a possible puddle.

"Yeah, he's very cute." I crossed my fingers behind my back. "Are you going out with him?"

"Not yet, my friend. Not yet. But I'm making it a top priority."

Lorelei gave me a searching look. "Unless you're thinking about throwing your hat in the ring?"

My face turned almost as red as the Exit sign over the door, and I tried to calculate how many steps away it was.

"Dani? Are you interested in him? What about that cute boyfriend I see you with?"

Tristan. His name is Tristan. And I'm a horrible human being.

"I… I wasn't planning on asking him to the party. He's busy anyway. Studies, work."

"So, are you interested in Cole or not?" Lorelei asked. "Sounds like the boyfriend might not be a boyfriend for long."

"I don't know any more what I want. Cole is really cute, and he makes me feel something I haven't felt with Tristan."

"Horny?" Lorelei laughed as she said it. "Cuz he does the same thing to me."

My stomach flipped a little. "I feel like a combination of butterflies, flu, and brain fog, like I can't control myself around him."

"Yesssssssss!" Lorelei hissed. "Same! What magic does he have over us?!?"

I felt better about her now, especially since she was feeling the same way. We were bonding in our lust over a guy. I felt the jealousy fade a bit, so I opened up to Lorelei.

"I don't know. I kissed him three minutes after meeting him the other night."

"I'm sorry, what? You kissed him already? I'm slacking."

"Twice. I kissed him twice. Don't know what came over me." I hung my head, ashamed.

"Girl, I am so proud of you! I've been wanting to do that ever since I noticed his lips."

She was proud of me and all I could think about was how I cheated on Tristan without a second thought.

"But I still have a boyfriend. And I shouldn't have done it. I never even think about Tristan when I'm around Cole."

"I'm telling you, he's got some magic in him. It's like he casts a spell over us."

"But just us? I mean, Sara doesn't feel like that when she's around him."

"Maybe just us. We'll ask some others at the party if they've noticed anything."

With that, she locked up the gallery, and I followed her upstairs to her apartment. I'd never been up there before, and it's amazing. Art hung everywhere, pottery sat on shelves, and a pile of sweaters rested on her hot pink couch.

"Here, choose one!"

There were six, each uglier than the next.

"Which one are you wearing?" I asked.

Lorelei let out a laugh and lifted a sweater folded on a turquoise beanbag chair. It was just as ugly as the six others, and I was a little relieved she wouldn't outshine me with a spectacular outfit.

Laughing, I chose a black sweater with a large, light-up snowman appliqué on the front. His outline had tiny LED lights, and his scarf was made entirely from red and green Christmas lights. It came with its own tiny battery pack. I turned the switch on, and the sweater came to life in front of me.

"Black leggings and combat boots and you'll be da belle of da ball." Lorelei kicked off her shoes. "Do you want a beer or something?"

"No thanks, I need to get home for dinner."

"No worries. Hey, listen, I know you're pretty young, right? What are you, twenty? Maybe I should warn you about that 'fun stuff' Cole is bringing. A bottle of vodka to make Jello shots and some coke. But you don't have to do anything if you don't want to. We're all a little older than you are, anyway. You're the baby of the bunch. I invited some of my friends, too, and nobody will even notice if you don't drink."

"Oh, I don't care, honest!" I blushed for the umpteenth time today. "And I'm nineteen. But I drink beer sometimes when Tristan comes over."

"Okay. I just wanted to make sure you wouldn't feel weird. I'll have some spiked seltzer here, which is tons better than beer. I hate beer. So try some of that if you want."

I thanked Lorelei for everything and walked home thinking about Cole and ugly sweaters and wondering what the hell a Jello shot was like.

CHAPTER 18

SARA

I had just taken a break from decorating the tree when Dani came home from work.

"Ooh, Sara, it looks so good."

"Thanks! It's getting there. I'm totally ignoring the back of the tree. Otherwise, I'd run out of ornaments. This tree is larger and taller than what we normally end up with from the farm."

I noticed the sweater in Dani's arms. "Whatcha got there?"

Dani held up the sweater by the shoulders to show it off. "But wait, there's more!" she cried, and hit the On button, giving me a glimpse of its true beauty.

"Wow. That should win a prize." I didn't want to insult her. But seriously.

"Ha! I know it's ugly. But it's so festive! And there will be a prize for the best ugly sweater."

"You're a shoo-in. Just don't spill anything on it, and not just because I'm worried that you'll get electrocuted. It would be a bitch to clean."

Dani looked at me with enormous eyes. "This can't really electrocute me, right?"

"I don't know," I said ominously. "Guess we'll find out."

"Sara!"

She ran up the stairs with Molly hot on her heels, apparently thinking Dani held a new dog toy. I heard her a moment later trying to convince the golden retriever the sweater was not, in fact, something to rip apart.

Erik found me standing still, mug in hand, staring at the finished Christmas tree with a critical eye.

"Hey, I'm going to heat up my leftovers. Are you hungry?"

"Famished. I worked up an appetite." I wiggled my eyebrows at my handsome husband-to-be.

"Same, baby. Same."

"Are you guys trying to make me move out?" Dani called from her room. "Because you're doing a great job of it."

"I meant I'm famished from decorating this tree!" I poked Erik in the ribs. "Your father, though…"

"Staaaaahhhhpppp." The anguished cry came from the top of the stairs.

Erik poked me back, and we walked to the kitchen arm in arm, Tank coming to life when he realized where we were heading.

Over our casual dinner, we discussed how and where furniture would be moved for our big day.

"You'll have Ethan to help, and his stepson. Maybe Lucas?"

"I'll be glad for the extra help. My back isn't what it used to be." Erik's face went slack and I looked at him in alarm. "I just sounded like my father. When did that happen? When did I get old, Sara?"

"Babe. You're a studly beast and absolutely in your sexual prime, no matter what anyone says."

"I was pretty studly earlier, wasn't I?"

"Ay Papi," I murmured.

Dani walked into the kitchen, holding her forehead. "I swear you guys really are trying to get me to move out."

Next house? More privacy.

CHAPTER 19

DANI

I played with hairstyles for the party. Maybe something funny, like pigtails or braids wrapped in ribbons. After an hour of trying different ideas, I gave up and decided I would go with whatever felt right on Saturday.

I thought about texting Tristan just to say hi and maybe mention the situation—the situation meaning Cole and the kisses. But the sick pit in my stomach made me throw that idea out the window. I scrolled social media until my guts felt firmer.

I can't do this much longer. The roller coaster of confusion, lust, shame and guilt made me squirm with unpleasant feelings all throughout my body. My guts churned and my stomach flipped, causing my anxiety to build.

I was going to have to deal with this sooner rather than later. The threat of a bathroom run in the middle of the party scared the hell out of me. I feel like there's two kinds of people in the world. Those who can poop anywhere, anytime, without a second thought. And those who will do anything to wait until they are home in their own bathroom. I am a firm member of the second group. Same with Sara. I'd prefer not to know what group my dad is in, but I had a pretty good guess.

Molly scratched at my closed bedroom door, and I opened it to see she had a leash in her mouth and a note tied with a Christmas ribbon around her neck.

Please walk me, Dani? Mommy and Daddy are busy smooching under the mistletoe and don't have time for me. Love, Molly.

"Are you kidding me right now?" I yelled. "What's gotten into you guys?"

My dad's voice came through the wall: "Mistletoe. And a hot fiancée."

Please. Save. Me.

I heated the leftover Thai from the refrigerator and carried it upstairs to my room because sitting at the kitchen table with the overly gooey lovebirds was just too awkward and cringey. I loved them, but I needed to figure out what I wanted to do with my life and what it would take to get my own place.

College just didn't appeal, but I know it's what's expected. I couldn't see the point of getting a degree if I didn't even know what I wanted to do. High school was okay, but the thought of nothing but classes, studying, and tests for four years made my head hurt. We had all finally agreed I would wait a year and work at the bookshop before going to college. It had been about eighteen months since I graduated, and even though nobody had said anything, I needed to tell them I was still unsure. I couldn't be the only person to feel this way. Lots of people don't go to college, right?

When I talked to Sara about this months ago, she told me to write down everything and anything that interested me, no matter what it was. My list was simple. Traveling. Animals. Charms &

Chapters. Reading. The Jersey shore. Hiking. Binge-watching Netflix shows. I saw nothing on that list that screamed career, unless I just stayed put at the shop.

I honestly enjoyed being at the bookshop. I loved unpacking new books and dusting the crystals, which Sara hated doing so it's a good thing I liked it. The customers were almost always nice.

I liked living here. This town was awesome. So many of our local customers have become friends. We have a real town square with churches and a stately courthouse. Small-town living surrounded by farmland and some of the best shopping—and the quirkiest stores around, if I did say so myself.

Since I didn't feel like watching TV, I put on some music, grabbed my headphones and the new King novel, and lost myself in a world only he can create so successfully.

I heard a weird noise from downstairs, a cross between a little dog's yippy bark and the howl of a werewolf, and called out, "Are you guys okay? What was that?"

Laughter rose from the first floor.

"Come see for yourself!" yelled Sara.

Sometimes this house was like a three-ring circus I fully expected to be cringing at whatever shenanigans they were up to. But I had to check it out. Plus, I heard that sound again, followed by Sara's hoot of laughter.

I found them on the couch, Sara straddling my father and holding his forehead down.

"Do I even want to know?"

Sara turned her head and clicked the pair of tweezers in her right hand.

"Your father requested I rid his eyebrows of some incredibly long curly white hairs."

"She's torturing me! It shouldn't hurt this much," my father whined.

"Erik. I can't get this done if you won't stop being a baby."

"How much longer? Can you stop here?"

"No. Babe. I can't stop here. One eyebrow is tamed. I don't understand why you don't have your barber trim them."

"Because I hate the way they feel when he does that. Pluck. Please, just get this over with."

A tear slipped out of the corner of Dad's left eye.

Sara took a huge breath and went back to her chore. I heard the yippy howl come out of my dad's mouth, but I still didn't know how he made that sound.

Sara rolled her eyes. "Oh my Goddess. Babe. Women do this all the time without the histrionics."

I left them to their plucking.

CHAPTER 20

SARA

After Dani went back upstairs and I finished making Erik cry, I mentioned the party she was planning on attending in a couple of days. "Lorelei invited a bunch of the local shop owners for an ugly sweater Christmas party this weekend."

"Cool. Let's go get sweaters tomorrow."

"Babe, we're not invited."

"We're shop owners, aren't we?"

"We're not young shop owners."

"Bullshit. Sixty is the new thirty." Erik's brow furrowed. "That's age discrimination."

"Well, whatever you want to call it, we're not invited. But Dani is, and so is Cole."

"Cole's not a shop owner."

"Yes, but he's incredibly cute and I'm pretty sure Dani is interested."

"I think we should crash it."

"The party? Are you serious?" I held my forehead with my palm. "Erik, babe, we're not crashing the party. Dani would disown us both."

"She'd never do that. It would mean living with her mother."

That made me laugh. "We're still not crashing it. Sometimes I think you live to mortify your daughter."

"Thanks to you, I have my daughter in my life to mortify. I often wonder how that summer would have played out if you hadn't been there. Dani was so miserable when her mom left her with me. I remember how she cried. It about broke my heart."

"I think you would have found your path together, even without me. It might have taken a little longer, but you both love each other. I just eased the awkwardness of those early days with my own awkwardness."

"There were some incredibly awkward moments." Erik poked at me. "Remember the lemonade?"

I leaned over and gave him a kiss. "Oh, yeah." It should have been a mortifying memory, with Erik catching sight of me mostly naked after I dumped a pitcher of lemonade all over myself, but I recalled the dang stickiness most of all.

"So, is Tristan officially history?"

"Not officially, but I think it might come soon. He'll be done with the semester after this week, so we'll see what next week brings."

I planned to use Lily's tarot cards to read more about Dani's situation. And a bigger spread than just the one card I had pulled. But it would have to be tomorrow morning first thing, or as soon as my brain woke up. That required tea, breakfast, and coffee. Anything happening before that sequence was completed, well, I wouldn't understand the message.

"C'mon, eyebrow boy, let's go upstairs. I have plans for you," I whispered.

Erik grabbed my hand, and we ran up the stairs together, laughing the entire way.

Dani was standing outside her bedroom door, headphones in hand, waiting for us.

"I could hear you even through my headphones. I swear these walls are made of paper."

Erik took the words right out of my mouth. "I suggest you turn your music up as loud as you can stand it, little girl. Cuz we're about to get funky up in here."

"Daaaaaaaaadohmygodstaaaahhhp."

It was all one word. I swear.

I offered to open for Dani the next morning because I wanted some time with the cards before any interruptions. Molly and I walked down to the shop together, enjoying the quiet streets before the hum of the day began. I started a pot of coffee and sat down with the drawstring bag I'd chosen to hold Lily's cards. It felt warm to the touch. That threw me, until I noticed cat hairs decorating the colorful bag. I looked over at Kat, who had her back to me and was happily eating her special kibble with gravy. She paused and glanced over her shoulder as if she knew I was looking her way. Blinking slowly, Kat then bowed her head and went back to her breakfast.

I brushed off the little black hairs, tugged open the drawstring, and held Lily's deck in my hands. The edges worn with age, the design on the back simple and faded. I felt the warmth flow through my fingers, and there was no way that was from Kat's butt. It was just like the warmth I'd felt from the touch of Lily's hand in Lavallette. Whenever I was overthinking something, which was more often than I liked to admit, my go-to meditation had been reliving those magical minutes when the outside world and all my troubles had faded away. Images of her beautiful face flashed through my brain, seeing once more how it had morphed from old to young and back again. I held Lily's deck to my heart, then shuffled it and set the intention for the reading.

I did a seven-card spread because I wanted more detailed guidance than a three- or five-card one would give me. The cards were in a horseshoe shape in front of me and I stared at them one by one, using my guidebook to understand what I was looking at.

The 7 of Cups. Her current position is her "emotional choices" card. This indicates that there are choices to be made but reminds her that not all that glitters is gold.

The Fool. Her "what she's expecting" card, showing the start of a new journey.

The 3 of Cups. Her "what she's not expecting" card, indicating she wasn't expecting the heartache of having to choose between two men.

Covering the 3 of Cups was the Magician Reversed on the left. A dishonest man, able to morph into whoever he needs to be to charm her, but don't trust him. On the right, the King of Wands. A hardworking, loyal man, filled with integrity but dull and not focused on romance.

The 5 of Cups. Her "soon to be known" card. This one indicates that she's looking at what's been lost and that she's feeling alone.

The Ace of Cups, showing a new relationship that will come when she's ready and healed.

Wow. I sat with that for a minute, going over my notes and guidebook and double-checking online to make sure I was reading it correctly.

Everything stuck with me and made complete sense in light of what I knew about Dani's situation. The nonstop chills running up the back of my neck told me the truth was in front of me. And the bonus: Kat jumping on the table and sitting directly on the Magician card.

I scratched her behind the ears, one of her favorite spots.

"She's going to go through some shit, isn't she?" I asked the cat, half expecting her to answer me. Instead, Kat pushed her head against my hand and looked into my eyes. A slow blink confirmed what I suspected.

My heart ached for what Dani had coming her way. At nineteen she was facing some hard choices, but I hoped she could understand that at the end there was a healed heart and a happily ever after.

I took a sip of my now cold coffee and made a face. I am not one of those die-hard coffee drinkers who can enjoy the precious beans cold. Hot and black, please. The microwave gave me what I wanted. Unfortunately, the first sip burned the roof of my mouth, and I ended up with a huge blister bubble, which my tongue refused to leave alone.

What a way to start the day.

CHAPTER 21

DANI

I sat at the table with Sara, Kat in my lap, and my jaw hanging almost to the floor.

"Holy crap, Sara. I have goosebumps all over."

"I know, right? I kept rechecking what I pulled, and it all jives."

"I mean, that's obviously Cole, isn't it?" I said, pointing to the Reversed Magician. "And the other is Tristan. Hardworking but dull."

"Hard to read any other way." Sara put her hand on my arm. "Just keep all this in mind, especially at Lorelei's party. I can't be there for you because, apparently, I'm an ancient hag, but I'm only just down the street if you need me. Or Dad."

I laughed at the ancient hag part. "I promise. And you're not an ancient hag. You're not even a hag. You're a…" I paused, weighing my options. "Crone."

Sara tipped her head to the right. "I'll take crone. In fact, I'll take that as a high compliment. Now you'll have to excuse me while I go conjure up some fresh coffee, get Molly fed, and cast a spell for lots of customers today."

Sara was no joke in that department. People started streaming in as soon as I switched the sign to Open. She just smiled smugly when I shook my finger at her.

The day flew by with steady customers, and Sara didn't leave early because we were simply too busy for her to leave me alone. The holidays were upon us, and it seemed as if everyone in town was stopping in to buy gifts and enjoy a hot cup of something. We offered gift wrapping, which was now my job because even though Sara was an artist, she couldn't wrap a present to save her life. She used too much tape and everything was crooked. She'd always end up with paper cuts and tape stuck to her hair. I had to rescue her so many times that I finally took on that chore. Like dusting the crystals.

Sara walked up to the wrapping station, where I was just finishing up with a customer. She had an armful of books and an equal number of incense boxes.

"These are for Verity; she's sitting in her favorite spot in the reading area with a cup of coffee while she waits, so no rush. She already paid for everything, and we don't close for another hour."

"Okay, I'll bring them out to her when I'm done. I'll put a sticky note on each one, so she knows what's in each wrapped package."

Sara gave me a thumbs-up and walked away, already moving on to the next customer at the register.

As I carefully folded and smoothed the festive paper around each edge and corner, I thought about the tarot reading. It was so undeniably clear, and that made it hard to ignore the warning about Cole. Like there weren't enough red flags already, this was just icing on the cake.

Should I step back and give Lorelei the green light? Forget that Cole gave me feelings I've never felt before? Or jump into bed with him and get it done? That last thought brought a wave of lust, shame, more lust, and some guilt.

Would that scratch your itch? my inner voice asked. Or would it lead you deeper?

I finished wrapping Verity's ten hardcovers and ten small boxes of incense and still had no simple answer about the Cole situation. My fingers were sore, and I was glad to see it was nearing closing time.

I grabbed one of our large, colorful canvas totes and carefully laid the festive packages inside. Lifting it, I realized it was probably too heavy for Verity to carry with one hand, so I transferred half to another tote. At least she'd balance. Verity traded me her empty coffee mug for the totes and lifted the bags like they were no heavier than that empty mug.

"What?" she asked. "Did you think I was feeble?" Verity *tsk*ed and handed me a crisp $20 bill. "I'm not. This is for you, Dani. Thank you for not letting Sara wrap these." She whispered, "She's a terrible gift wrapper."

"Don't worry, Verity. I've got you."

We exchanged a conspiratorial look, and Verity touched her finger to the side of her nose. I nodded like I knew what that meant and touched my nose in return. Verity smiled, saluted me, and left the shop with her two canvas bags in tow.

The day was so busy right until closing that I didn't realize Cole had never come in. It's unusual for us to not have a delivery of some type, especially at this time of year. I wasn't sure if my concern was out of missing a delivery or missing Cole. The thump of blood rushing between my legs just from thinking about him stopped me in my tracks, lightheaded.

"You ok, Dani?" Sara's voice pierced through the cotton in my brain.

I sank into the comfortable chair Verity had just vacated. "Yeah, I just got a little dizzy."

"Have you eaten anything since lunch?"

"No," I admitted. "I just forgot."

Sara clucked her tongue and went into the back room to get me a candy bar out of her secret stash. We all know about it but pretend we don't.

"Eat this. And drink some water."

"Yes, Step-Monster ma'am."

I didn't think it was a low blood sugar issue; I think it was a Cole issue. But I'll never turn down a candy bar. I love chocolate as much as Sara. I chewed the yummy caramel, nougat, nut, and chocolate concoction as I locked the front door and switched the sign from Open to Closed. It was only 5:00 p.m., but it was already quite dark, and the temperature had dropped noticeably since I had walked in this morning.

"Better?" Sara asked.

"Much. Thanks."

"Getting excited about Saturday night? Only two days away!"

"I was more excited before, but now I have this weird feeling in my stomach every time I think about Saturday. Like ever since the reading."

"Follow your gut. If you don't want to go, don't go! It's really as simple as that."

"Why does life have to be this complicated?" I whined.

"Oh, baby girl. You ain't seen nothing yet." Sara walked away humming a tune very off-key and very not caring.

CHAPTER 22

SARA

Dammit, I had an earworm now and I'd never get rid of it. I only remembered a small bit of the song, so it repeated every three seconds in my brain. Erik's sure cure for this was to recite the lyrics to "The Girl from Ipanema" out loud.

When that failed, as it usually did, I turned on the kitchen radio. You'll never guess what song was playing. I'd say what are the chances, but with me the odds were actually pretty good for some type of magical weirdness being involved. At least I remembered the words now.

"Ooh, BTO!" cried Erik as he danced into the kitchen from the dining room. He grabbed me and we boogied around the kitchen until both dogs howled and Dani thumped the floor in her bedroom.

Giggling, Erik turned down the volume and drew me in for a kiss.

"This is quieter," he murmured into my mouth, then slid his tongue along my neck before returning to my lips. By this point, my legs were rubbery, and I wrapped my arms around his neck to keep from sliding to the ground. Just hearing his voice made me want him.

He grabbed my butt and lifted me onto the counter. My arms were still around his neck, my legs wrapped around his waist, and his lips nibbled my earlobe. He expertly maneuvered around my hoop earrings, and I silently thanked my grandmother for handing down her large earlobes to me. I much prefer them to her wide, flat butt, which my poor brother got.

Erik's hips ground into me and I thought we were going to have to move this to our bedroom. But Erik blew an *oof* sound into my mouth and broke away, laughing.

"Molly. Must you? Still?" he asked.

From the first time they met, Molly had greeted Erik with a nose jab to the crotch or butt, whichever was presented to her.

"You will not use that counter to prep dinner, right?" Dani asked, coming into the kitchen and taking in the scene in front of her. "Let me get the bleach wipes out of the pantry."

"Hilarious," I said as I slid off the counter. That's a long drop for someone with such short legs. "But not a bad idea."

Her gag was worth it.

Lying in bed that night, I told Erik about the tarot reading.

"It really was so apropos to her situation. I just hope she sees the guidance it offered and heeds the warning. It gave us both chills."

"I'll talk to her tomorrow. Or maybe I should take Cole aside and tell him to back off."

"Oh, that would go over really well with your daughter," I said sarcastically. "I can hear her already."

"Yeah. I can too," he admitted. "But that won't stop me if I need to do that. I am not scared of her."

I looked at him and raised an eyebrow. I idly wondered whether Cynthia had regained her ability to do that yet.

"Okay. I'm a little scared of her. I mean, she's a smart cookie, she's levelheaded, and she thinks fast. But I'm still going to talk to her about it." He leaned over and kissed me on the nose. "Sleep well, baby."

Two seconds later, he snored directly in my face. I popped my earplugs in and played a few games of solitaire on my tablet before calling it a night.

Dani leaned on the register and waved me over when I walked into the shop the next day.

"Did you know Dad was going to talk to me about Cole and your reading?"

"I did. He insisted."

"I'm not a baby and I'm not being careless. He just doesn't trust me to make good decisions."

"It's normal for a dad to worry about his little girl. No matter how old you get, that will never change."

"I'm nineteen! I do nothing wrong. I don't go anywhere, just work and come home. He never did this about Tristan. He's being way too overprotective."

Dani's defiant tone caught me by surprise. A pushback. And of course it's over a guy. "It's not that he doesn't trust you."

"He doesn't trust Cole. That's it, right?"

"Well, that's a good part of it. He doesn't want you to get hurt. And he doesn't know this guy from Adam. Honestly, neither do you. Plus, you're going to be at a party with him, and you can't be too careful these days around people you don't know."

Dani's scowl told me to back off. I could read her loud and clear ever since we met. I moved away before I was tempted to say anything else. I knew she had a good head on her shoulders, but that didn't make me worry any less.

CHAPTER 23

DANI

With both Dad and Sara coming at me about Cole, my mood turned sour, and I had to work hard at keeping a pleasant look on my face so I wouldn't scare the customers. Sara always says nothing kills a sale quicker than a resting bitch face.

It didn't help that it was a Friday evening, and I was date-less and might as well be boyfriend-less too. I kicked the side of the counter absentmindedly. I hadn't heard from Tristan. His exams should be over soon, yet he hadn't texted me. Wondering if I should even buy him a Christmas present, I tried picturing his face. I couldn't focus it in my brain, so I opened my photo gallery and looked at our most recent selfie, which we took together just a couple of weeks ago. He was just as cute as Cole but in a clean-cut football hero/Ken doll way compared to Cole's cute in a bad boy way. You knew just by looking at Cole that he'd be a good kisser. That he'd be an awesome friend with benefits. That he would probably break your heart when the friends with benefit thing didn't work for you and you caught feelings. While Tristan was safe and reliable (usually) and while the thought of him didn't make my entire body start fire like the thought of Cole did, I knew Tristan wouldn't break my heart. And maybe that was the problem. My internal conflict wasn't because I was so sure of Tristan's love for me; it was because I didn't think I loved him enough that my heart would break without him.

$\sim$

I opened Charms & Chapters Saturday morning so that I could leave early to get ready for Lorelei's party. The day crawled by with the knowledge that I wouldn't see Cole until this evening. Even a steady customer stream didn't help speed the day ahead. I handled the register while Sara restocked, and if someone needed gift wrapping, she relieved me so I could manage that.

At 3:00 p.m. Sara shooed me out the door. "Your dad is coming down right away to help me, so go on home. If you need help getting ready, just call me, but you have your outfit all planned out, right?"

"I do. But I'll yell if I think of anything. The party doesn't start for a few hours, so you'll be home before I leave anyway."

Just as I was walking out the door, I heard a customer at the counter ask Sara where I was going, and I paused.

"She's heading home. Can I help you with something?"

"I want to buy this book, but I was hoping to have it gift wrapped." Even from the doorway, I could see the chagrined look on the customer's face.

"I can do that for you."

"Oh." The woman's voice was flat. "Maybe I'll just come back tomorrow if she's here."

"I'm really that bad, aren't I?" Sara asked.

"I'm sorry, Sara, but I remember last year's wrapping job and I'd prefer that not happen again."

By this time, I'd walked back to the counter and took the book from Sara's hands.

"It will take me no time at all. Be right back."

I'm not sure who looked more grateful.

~

Once I got home and grabbed a snack to quiet my stomach, I took a long, hot shower and washed my hair. I have a body wash that smells like coconut and a shampoo that matches. Maybe Cole would like to crack my coconut. I chuckled to myself and grabbed my razor to rid myself of leg hair. I wasn't planning on anyone noticing whether my legs were shaved under my black leggings. But there's always the slight possibility someone might get that far. Not just *someone*. Cole. Cole might get that far. The familiar flush of lust and shame rushed through my body as I imagined Cole running his hands over my smooth legs. Or his lips. I held on to the grab bar in the shower. Feeling completely under whatever spell Cole was casting, I shaved until I was smooth, and after getting out of the shower, I lotioned my still-damp skin.

The black leggings were easy. I had at least twenty-three pairs. The boots were Sara's. The Christmas sweater was a little scratchy, so I put a long-sleeved black T-shirt first. I wasn't ready to put the sweater on yet though. Hair and makeup came next. I blew my long hair dry and pulled it up in a clip to do my makeup, which wasn't much. Some blush, a little eyeliner, and mascara. Back to the hair. I decided on two braids, one on each side, but I wanted to add a ribbon into the braids. Checking the time, I realized Sara was probably home, so I ran downstairs, finding my dad on the couch.

"Is that how you're going to the party?"

"Dad. No. Of course not. Where's Sara? Is she home yet?"

"How come you never need me? I can help too, you know."

I rolled my eyes. "Okay, I need two long pieces of ribbon. Preferably red. But the red must match the red in the sweater. If they're glittery, even better."

"Sara!" my dad called towards the kitchen. "Dani needs you."

"That's what I thought."

~

It only took Sara three minutes in her studio to find the perfect matching ribbon and—huge score—there were tiny bells attached to it. I put the sweater on before doing my hair so it wouldn't catch on anything. I tried a number of different options, from weaving in the ribbons to wrapping them around the braids, but nothing seemed to work. Finally I determined that the braids needed to go, and I was happy to see they left me with some pretty sweet waves. I wound the jingly ribbons around the hair ties that held my two ponytails. That did the trick, and I liked it better. If the jingling drove me up a wall, I could always take the ribbons out. I was feeling cute even in the ridiculous sweater, so I snapped a selfie and posted it on my IG. I closed my phone and slipped it into that perfectly placed pocket on the side of my leggings. One last glance in the mirror told me I looked ready, so I went downstairs to show Dad and Sara.

They gave me the proper worship and took a few pictures before my dad lightly grabbed my shoulders and pulled me to his chest.

"Kiddo, I know I don't have to tell you to be careful. I trust you to do the right thing and remember how old you are. I want you to always be aware of your surroundings."

"Dad. I'm literally going to be two blocks away. I know most of the people who will be there, by sight at least. I'll be fine."

"And I'm sure you will be. But just be careful. Okay?"

"I will. Stop worrying."

I know it was normal for him to worry because he loves me. Plus, he knew Cole would be there. And it was possible Sara had filled him in just a little about my feelings for Cole.

Then Sara piped in. "We're just a scream away from rescuing you from whatever happens."

"Are you walking down?" Dad asked.

"Yup."

"Are you going to drink?"

"Dad, I have had beer before with Tristan. You know that. I don't hide it from you. I might have a hard seltzer or something, I don't know. But I will not get drunk or anything."

My father's face got very serious.

"Remember, you're not legal to drink. Not to mention, you've seen firsthand what alcohol can do to a family, what it can do to me. You've been to enough meetings with me to understand how easy it can be to lose yourself."

"Dad, I know. I remember. I'm not going to get drunk. Just planning to have some fun and hopefully win the ugly sweater contest." I got on my tiptoes and kissed his nose. "I'll be fine. Honest."

"I have full faith in you. I don't have full faith in the people surrounding you. So just be aware."

I looked at the clock and grabbed my coat off the hook by the door.

"I love you both. Have fun without me here." I was going to follow that up with "don't do anything I wouldn't do," but that might have earned me another lecture from my dad. Or worse, some gross, cringey suggestion of what they actually planned to do when I wasn't home.

I was halfway to Lorelei's when my leg vibrated with an incoming text message. The text was from Tristan, so I stopped to read it.

TRISTAN

Hey, do you have a sec to talk?

It was like all the men in my life wanted to keep me from this party. But I hit Dial because I wasn't about to spend my evening wondering what he wanted. I barely got a hello out when he started speaking.

"Dani, we have to talk. I hate doing this right before Christmas, but I have to."

My body started to shake a bit, predicting what was coming next. "Have to do what? Are you breaking up with me? Right now? Over the phone?"

My heart was pounding. The tears were standing by, still unsure if they were needed.

"I'm sorry, Dani. Honest. I care about you a lot, but life just isn't making it easy for us, and I think we'll both be better off in the long run."

What the hell was I feeling? Sad? Mad? Relieved that I didn't have to tell him about kissing Cole? Glad the shame pit could go away? Happy he had decided this for me? I couldn't put my finger on which one was right. Or maybe they all were.

"Wow. Was not expecting this tonight. I don't know what to say except if that's what you want, then I wish you the best in the future. Have a good life."

With those words, I burst out crying. He said three sentences, and we were done. Like the last eighteen months never happened. I was dumped and alone right before Christmas.

"Dani—"

I hit the End Call button and wiped my nose on a tissue I found in my coat pocket. I didn't even care if it was clean. I was going to have to pass the gallery so I could run into the bookshop and try to repair my makeup. Then I would not let myself cry until after the party. I promised myself another long, hot shower where I could sob if I wanted. Funny thing, I still wasn't sure I needed to sob. I was hurt, but honestly, wasn't I feeling the same way? And I was the one who kissed another guy. Twice. I was the one who dressed herself from head to toe intending to capture Cole's attention. I didn't deserve to sob. Maybe I'd cry a little. But not sob. Tristan was an excellent learning experience.

I checked my phone again when I got to Charms & Chapters. Nine texts, two missed calls, and one voicemail from Tristan. The texts were all the same. Dani please call me. Dani I still care about you. I just think we need time apart. Dani don't ignore me please. And on and on.

Nothing I felt like handling right now. Let him worry. I didn't listen to his voicemails.

After cleaning up my smudged makeup in our tiny bathroom, I checked on Kat and filled her bowls. Litter box would have to wait —no way was I cleaning that before the party. I left my winter coat here, figuring I would just freeze for a few minutes until I got inside Lorelei's apartment.

I scrunched my wavy pigtails and jingled my happy ass to the party.

CHAPTER 24

SARA

"What are you doing, babe?"

I looked up from my phone where I'd been doom-scrolling for more than a few minutes.

"Nothing worthwhile. Got any ideas?"

Erik raised one eyebrow and cocked his head to the stairs.

Laughing, I climbed into his lap, straddling him.

"What's your rush? We'll have plenty of time."

"You're a sexy wench and I want to spend all that time ravishing your body with my mouth."

I almost kicked him in the chin trying to jump off his lap backwards.

"Sorry, babe, but I need to jump in the shower if you're going to be putting your mouth anywhere on my body right now."

"I'll meet you in the bedroom." He stood, his wolf smile creasing his gorgeous face, and we went upstairs arm in arm.

By 10:00 p.m. we were back cuddling on the couch with just the Christmas tree lit, listening to music and talking about the wedding.

Erik looked at the time and let out a little sigh. "I'm worried about her, Sara. I don't know why. This feels different."

I'm usually intuitive with Dani, but nothing specific was nagging me. I tried tapping into our special brain messaging and sent her questioning vibes. Nothing happened. I sent her a quick text asking if everything was going okay. No answer. I would normally trust that all was well, but Erik's concern troubled me.

My phone vibrated with a text from Tristan's mom, Lisa.

> LISA
>
> Hey sorry to bother you this late. Hope you're up. Tristan just told me he broke up with Dani. Is she ok? She's not answering his calls or texts.

Well, crap. That must have happened after she left the house. I felt my worry ramp up.

"Babe, I just got a text from Lisa. Tristan broke up with Dani tonight."

"Oh man. Why didn't she tell us? Did it happen after she left? Must have, she didn't seem upset before she left." Erik held his head with his hand. "I knew something wasn't right. I felt it. I can't believe you didn't."

I couldn't believe that either. Maybe I was just too caught up with wedding plans, holidays, and the shop and all wrapped up in Self. I felt a pang of regret. Did Dani need me, and I'd been too self-involved to notice? I resolved to correct that tomorrow morning. There was no way I was letting this relationship become compromised.

I answered Lisa, told her we did not know it happened, and said Dani was not home. I promised to keep her posted on Dani's mental state when she got back.

Poor Dani. I knew things were trailing off with Tristan, but I expected Dani to be the one ending the relationship for good. It wouldn't be the first time they broke up, either. I'd been through it before with her. She would cry and be sad and then the next time it would be her doing the breaking up. So I wasn't hugely concerned about her. But I wasn't worry-free either.

We agreed neither of us could sleep a wink until Dani got home, so I made us both a cup of black tea.

And we waited.

CHAPTER 25

DANI

The music coming from Lorelei's apartment above the gallery was loud enough that I heard it from the sidewalk outside. I wondered if Cole had arrived yet and realized I didn't know what kind of car he drove when he wasn't in his delivery truck. There were quite a few vehicles parked along the street on both sides—more than usual—telling me the party was well underway. Good. I needed a little fun to get my mind off Tristan. I was free to be with Cole if I wanted, without the guilt I'd been feeling until this point.

I clicked the On button so that my sweater would light up and rang the bell to Lorelei's upstairs apartment. Several voices spoke together through the camera near the doorbell.

"C'mon up, door's open!" Laughter followed.

I took a deep breath and opened the door. The stairs were long, narrow, and steep and not well lit, so I took my time going step by step. My dad would be so proud of my great step work. That thought made me chuckle through my hurt feelings and dashed self-confidence, which was rearing its ugly head.

With each step, my pigtails jingled, and I hoped the other

guests looked as ridiculous as I felt I did. I thanked the Universe that Sara was clumsy and never wore heels, so the boots I borrowed were flat. At the top of the stairs, another door led into Lorelei's place.

There were at least fifteen people there already, and the party seemed to be in full swing. Current pop music played from speakers hung from the ceiling in the corners of the living room. A folding table in the middle of the room was set up for beer pong, and Lorelei's kitchen counter was littered with bottles of alcohol and more than a few baggies of weed.

I recognized several locals from other downtown shops and wandered over to say hello. Lorelei wasn't in sight and the other guests must have been her friends, since they didn't look familiar. Everyone I saw had on an ugly sweater, but none of them lit up like mine, so I felt like I had a leg up in that department.

The doorbell rang and a few people rushed the button to yell "come on up." The way they all laughed and patted each other on the back made me smile. They seemed to have made a game out of it.

Lorelei had the place decorated for the holidays. That she got all that done in one day amazed me. When I picked up my sweater, there was nothing showing Christmas in her apartment. Twinkling colored lights now draped every wall and surrounded each window. Her tree was tall and pencil thin and glowed with white lights. I looked around and envied her big time. This is what I wanted. My own place. The ability to decorate it any way I wanted. Friends. Privacy. Music without having to wear headphones.

"Hey everyone, I'm back!" Lorelei walked into the apartment with a bag of ice from the liquor store down the street.

"Lorelei!" the doorbell gamers called out in unison and then patted each other's backs again.

She looked incredible, just like she always did. Her braids were wrapped in silver bands, jingle bells, and colorful ribbons.

My hand flew to my pigtails and my last-minute wrap job. Not nearly as cool as what Lorelei had done.

Her sweater was tie-dyed red and green in a swirly pattern that could make you dizzy if you stared long enough. Black ankle boots and skin-tight leggings completed her outfit. Despite the fact that we were wearing the same basic thing, we looked nothing alike. Her body was curvy and her energy screamed sex.

My smile froze as Cole stepped through the door behind her, bottle in hand and looking edible in a Christmas sweater vest and jeans. The gamers yelled out Cole's name and he walked over to them to help pat backs.

He's been here already. He went to the liquor store with her. Cole pulled a tiny baggie from his jeans pocket and dangled it at the group. The patting of backs started all over again. I considered joining them, since they seemed to be having more fun than I was. The other shop people were nice, but definitely not as spirited as Lorelei's friends.

I searched out Lorelei to say hello even though I was feeling a certain way about how natural she and Cole looked together.

"Hey, Dani!" she said. "You must have come in while I was out. Welcome! Did you meet my friends yet?"

"The back patters?" I laughed. "They seem like they're having fun."

Lorelei chuckled at my description and led me over to the group, which still included Cole.

"Dani!" Cole said, putting his arm around me.

He had his arm around me. Just me. Not Lorelei. I stepped a little closer and swung my arm around his waist while he introduced me to Lorelei's friends, pointing at each one with the little baggie filled with white powder still in his hand. The bottle he'd brought had already disappeared into the kitchen bar area, taken from him by an enthusiastic partygoer.

"Nice to meet you all. You make a great greeting committee!"

My compliment made them all pat each other's back again

before one of them produced and offered a fresh dollar bill, rolled up tightly. Cole gave me a questioning look. I shook my head and stepped back to let them at it. He shrugged and slid a credit card from his back pocket, bending down to divide the snowy powder into several skinny lines on the table.

I was curious about coke, but not curious enough to try it. My dad would have had heart failure if he ever knew. He'd probably pitch a fit just knowing there was coke at the party. But I certainly wasn't planning to tell him.

Seeing Cole in his natural state, out of his work role, made him even more attractive to me. He not only looked like a bad boy, but he was the real deal. His jeans hugged him perfectly. Black cowboy boots. He wore a long-sleeved black shirt under the Christmas vest, which was red-and-white candy cane themed, buttoned and form-fitting. I thought about licking his candy cane, which made me flush and cough.

His eyes were bright when he turned around towards me. "Let me get you something to drink."

I was afraid I would choke if I tried to speak, so I nodded gratefully.

"Beer? Wine? A shot? What's your pleasure?" Cole led me to the kitchen.

Well, my pleasure would be you, obviously. Just the thought of pleasure and Cole together gave me ripples of lust, and my brain shut off the part still thinking about the loss of Tristan.

"Do you like this?" he asked, pointing to a punch bowl filled with a foamy orange liquid.

"I've never tried it. What does it taste like?"

"Here. Find out for yourself." With that, he filled a shot sized plastic cup and handed it to me. "Bottoms up."

I raised the cup to my lips and Cole put his finger under my chin and lifted it, my mouth opening automatically. The drink poured in quickly and down my throat, choking me. I coughed and gagged as the alcohol burned on the way down.

"You okay?!?" Cole laughed. "Do you like it?"

The alcohol sent a warmth throughout my body. Or maybe that feeling was just because I had Cole's full attention.

"I like it."

"You'll like it even better after another cup."

I heard my father's voice in my head. He would be seriously disappointed that I was about to have a second drink so soon after arriving at the party. He'd probably be seriously angry, too.

But I deserved this. I needed something to make me feel better. I started to consider everything I'd been going through lately. Aimless after 18 months here and no plans for the future. Dumped over the phone by an absent, and honestly boring, boyfriend. Spending Christmastime with a front-row seat to two old people falling more in love and celebrating by getting married. Not to mention those paper-thin walls that gave me no place to be truly alone. If having another drink gives me more time with Cole, even a few more minutes with him smiling at me and touching my face, sending warmth to all my extremities, then I'm going to drink. What could one more shot do?

A lot would be the answer. I was such a lightweight, having only had a beer here or there, and I found out quickly that one more shot did quite a lot to me. I noticed I was suddenly a little unsteady on my feet. I jingled away from Cole to the nearest chair, wanting to swing my hips alluringly but sure I'd never make it without tipping over if I did.

"Dani, are you okay?" one of the shop owners asked. "You look a little odd."

"Fine. I'm fine. Honest." And I was fine. Thanks to the alcohol, I felt as if I could do anything. Except maybe walk. And speak intelligently. But I liked it. I liked the warmth. The way things were a little out of focus really appealed to me right now.

Cole walked over to me and bent down to say something. "I'm watching you," he whispered in my ear.

The feeling of his breath against my skin made my nipples hard, and my stomach lurched. Why did I always react to him like that? I want him to touch me. I want him to do lots of stuff to me. I don't want to puke or, God forbid, something else every time he gets close to me.

"Why are you watching me?" I choked out.

"The shots. Lorelei just told me to stop giving you shots, that you don't really drink." Cole moved away from my ear and faced me directly. "So, I'm watching you to make sure you're okay."

His lips were right there in front of me. Just inches from my mouth. The turmoil in my stomach subsided and just when I was absolutely positive I wouldn't puke, he kissed me.

"I'm just fine," I murmured against his lips. To my delight, I felt Cole's tongue against my teeth, and I opened my mouth to give him full access. My entire body shuddered with pleasure as he sank to his knees in front of me without breaking contact with my lips.

Everything around me disappeared except Cole, shrinking away as my focus narrowed only to him. I didn't care that there were over a dozen people right outside our bubble. I just wanted this moment to last forever. He wouldn't be kissing me like this if he didn't want me as much as I wanted him.

"Okay, my turn!" a female voice cried.

Cole pulled away, laughing, leaving me looking like a fish out of water, gasping and eyes bugging.

He stood and kissed a girl standing under a spray of mistletoe Lorelei held aloft.

"Did you enjoy that?" Lorelei asked me, a sly smile on her face.

My brain couldn't form words yet, so I nodded and blinked slowly.

Someone else called out and Lorelei moved to hold the mistletoe over another girl's head. Cole slid his hand behind her neck and laid a kiss just as deep as ours on her mouth.

What the hell was going on here? Was Cole a party favor? At first it was just Lorelei's friends, people I didn't know, but by then even the other shop owners were giggling and waving to Lorelei to bring the mistletoe to them.

Some guy walked by my chair and offered me a lit joint. My first thought was why not? I wasn't sure if I could drink much more alcohol without puking, but I needed to do something because everything going on in my head was freaking overwhelming right now. Maybe weed would quiet all these feelings. I had already disappointed my dad and Sara anyway, so "why not?" seemed like a proper response to me. The shots had given me balls, and I plucked the joint from his hand like a veteran stoner.

The drag I took was not like a veteran stoner, though, and I thought my lungs were going to fly out of my mouth with every cough that followed.

"You okay, pretty mama?" the guy with the joint asked.

Why were people constantly asking me if I was okay? I was fine. But that word brought up the memory of something my dad always said. *FINE* stands for fucked up, insecure, neurotic, and empty. Maybe a couple of those fit me right now.

Tears streamed from my eyes as I tried to suppress another cough.

I nodded and took another hit of the joint because, other than the cough, I felt nothing. And for once, nothing felt good. Again, the words *why not* echoed through my fuzzy brain. I got more of this second hit into my lungs, and a huge plume of smoke came out of my mouth on the next cough.

"Thanks. I'm good." I wasn't sure I could stand though. "Would you be able to get me some water?" I cleared my raw throat and coughed again. The coughing made me feel a little shaky, and I was feeling strange.

"Sure thing, pretty girl. Be right back."

I looked around at the other partygoers. The group of shop owners, people I was familiar with, was still standing near the Christmas tree. A few people I didn't recognize were seated nearby on a couch and the welcoming committee folks were engaged in an apparently fierce game of beer pong on the table nearby. I pulled my phone from my pocket to see what time it was. 10:31 p.m. I noticed a few more missed texts from Tristan, and one from Sara asking if I was okay. I debated answering that one because I didn't know if I could sound normal or if she would get suspicious. My head was vibrating, and my hands were shaking. I felt like I'd just had five cups of coffee.

I felt a hand on my back and realized the joint guy was holding a bottle of water out to me. I tried to uncap it, but my hands seemed to be useless, and I pointed the bottle back at him for help. Noticing that joint guy was kind of cute, I tried to arrange my face into something that would pass as a smile. A sexy smile, if possible. Screw Cole for kissing all those girls.

"Thank you," I croaked, and took a long pull on the bottle of water. Ohmygod, that was life-giving. I could feel the water as it flowed down my throat and pictured it hitting my stomach like a waterfall in the rainforest. I wondered where the bathroom was, just in case I had to pee. Walking was going to be an issue, though. My mind wandered off, and I forgot what we were talking about. Were we talking?

"You're welcome, mama. What's your name?" Cute Joint Guy asked, taking a drag on the joint he'd taken back from me. "I'm Jay."

I had to think about my name. What was my name? Ohmygod, what was my name?

"Dani." Phew. It came back to me. "I'm Dani. Danielle."

"Nicetomeetchoo," he said, and I swear it all came out as one word.

His face was a little fuzzy, and I could feel my heart pound.

"I think I'm having a heart attack," I said to him. At least, I think I said that out loud. Minutes seemed to pass before he responded.

"Baby girl, you are not having a heart attack. I promise. Just breathe with me. C'mon, let's go somewhere quieter and we'll breathe and enjoy the high."

"No, I pretty sure I'm having a heart attack." It was beating so hard and fast, and now I was trying not to hyperventilate.

Jay laughed and helped me stand. "You can trust me. You are not having a heart attack. I'm going to prove it to you."

I wondered how he was going to do that and why he wasn't calling an ambulance.

"C'mon, pretty girl. I'm going to make you feel so good your head's gonna spin." Jay's voice sank through the fog that had replaced my brain.

"Dani, you okay?" Cole asked as we walked by, me being held up by Jay's arms mostly.

"She's good, my man. I've got her."

"I didn't ask you. I asked Dani."

"She's feeling a little under the weather right now," Jay said. "How about you leave her alone for a minute?"

"I'm having a heart attack, Cole."

"What? What do you mean?" Cole's voice got very serious.

"She's not having a heart attack, man; she took two colossal hits off some strong weed, and she just thinks she is."

"Is that what happened, Dani?"

"I did, but this is a heart attack. I'm positive. I can't breathe."

"You're breathing," Cole said.

Jay's arms tightened around me. "I'm just trying to make her feel better. I can calm her down."

"Yeah, I'm sure. Hit on someone else, buddy. I'll take care of Dani."

I felt Jay's hand loosen on my arm as he heeded the warning, and I swayed towards Cole, needing someone to help hold me upright.

"She's all yours, man. It's all good. I got her primed for you."

"Asshole," Cole muttered.

Jay waved and walked away, taking another pull off his joint.

"I think I'm having a heart attack, Cole."

"Dani, you're not. Let me listen to your heart."

And he put his ear to my chest. The little twinkling lights on the front of my sweater surrounded his head, and he looked so good. There's no way he couldn't hear that in my heartbeat.

"You smell good. I meant to tell you that before when I kissed you under the mistletoe," Cole whispered into my chest.

Coconut for the win. I hoped I would remember this. All of this. Even the fuzzy parts.

"Thank you. I'm having a heart attack."

He stood up and gazed into my eyes. He looked amused. "Dani, you're fine. You're high. It's normal."

"All of you are going to be sorry when I drop dead in the middle of the party."

That made Cole laugh out loud, and he grabbed my pigtails to draw me to him.

"Do you trust me enough to believe me you're fine?"

"Oh, I'm fine. I'm fucked up and insecure, but I'm not neurotic or empty."

"What are you talking about?" Cole asked. "How fucked up are you? We haven't even had the ugly sweater contest. Do you think you'll make it?"

I thought about it. "I have to pee. The shots made me woozy, and the joint gave me a heart attack."

"You're adorable. I'll show you where the bathroom is."

Cole pointed to a purple door, and luckily it was unoccupied.

After taking care of business and washing my hands, I stared at my face in the mirror. I looked... fuzzy. I still felt lightheaded, and my tongue felt like the Sahara Desert. I'd lost my bottle of water somewhere, so I cupped my hands under the faucet and drank cold sink water until my mouth felt normal and I could swallow without my trachea sticking to itself.

Cole knocked on the door. "You okay, Dani?"

I wished people would stop asking me that.

123

"Good, I'm good. I'll be out in a minute." Maybe another shot would make me feel better. My heart had finally stopped pounding quite so loud, but I wanted more of that woozy feeling. That felt good. Plus, Cole would be the one pouring it, and that might be worth it.

Maybe I wasn't having a heart attack after all.

One more shot turned into two more shots, because why not? And the woozy feeling returned with a vengeance. Cole's face swam in and out of focus, and I reached my hand out to steady his head.

"Stop moving, you're making me dishy."

"Dishy?" Cole hooted.

"You know what I mean. Ditzy."

"Oh, you're ditzy now?"

"No. Sara is ditzy. I am not ditzy." I felt bad for a minute throwing Sara under the bus like that, but let's face the facts. "Dizzy. Stop moving."

"I'm not moving, Dani. You're moving."

I booped his nose, which I considered a personal feat in light of his swaying. "You're hot."

"And you're drunk. Where's your water?"

I shrugged my shoulders. Cole grabbed a bottle from a tub of ice and opened it for me.

"Here. Drink."

I did as directed.

"I think I want to go home." I hiccuped and then started crying for some reason.

Lorelei came over and asked, "Dani? Are you okay?"

Was this ever going to stop? My head hurt, and now I just wanted to crawl into bed and forget this night ever happened.

"I'm okay, I just want to go home." I sniffed and sipped my water.

"I don't think that would be a good idea. You are still drunk, and I guarantee Sara and your dad are waiting up."

That made me cry again. "I'll go to the shop until I feel better. I just don't want to stay here anymore. Sorry."

Cole came to my rescue once again. "I'll walk you over there and make sure you're okay."

I thanked Lorelei and ducked out the door before anyone could stop me. I crossed my fingers that the other shop owners wouldn't tell Sara details about my behavior at the party. Cole followed me and grasped the back of my sweater before I got to the stairs.

"Let me get in front of you. In case you fall, I can catch you."

I hated to tell him I already fell. The first day I met him I fell, both literally and figuratively. As he brushed by me to get in front, I felt my heart pound again.

Breathe, Dani. Breathe.

I closed my eyes for a second to steady myself, but that made the stairway swirl all around me. Were we having an earthquake?

"Dani, open your eyes. The spinning will stop if you open your eyes."

Cole's voice sounded serious, so I obeyed him. But he was wrong. Everything continued to swirl and his arms reached out to hold me up when all I wanted to do was lie down.

"I need help," I said, and burst out crying again.

Just like he did the night we met, Cole picked me up. He made his way sideways down the narrow stairs. The spinning feeling left me, and the horny feeling returned. Tightening my arms around his neck, I whispered in his ear a breathy thank-you.

"Hey, I feel responsible, and I never should have given you those other shots. I feel bad."

My brain was too foggy to remember he'd said that after the first two shots as well.

Cole put me down at the bottom of the stairs, and we left the building. A quick walk down the alley and sidewalk brought us to Charms & Chapters. It felt so good to be out of the cold and in a place I felt safe. Kat stood up in her bed and started hissing and spitting as soon as she caught sight of Cole.

I picked her up and took her with me to the bathroom. Who knows what she might do to him if I left him alone with her? I splashed some water on my face, peed, and washed my hands. Still drunk. Definitely still drunk. Since I wasn't sure what part of me was drunk and what part was high, I blamed everything on the shots. And I did not like how I felt. At first it had felt good. Very good. And then it didn't.

Then I puked. With no warning. Holy crap, I'm glad the toilet was right next to me. I held my pigtails out of the water with one hand and grasped the edge of the bowl with the other. I'm also very glad Sara loves to clean bathrooms because ours was always sparkling. If I must puke in a toilet, I want it to be one of Sara's.

"Dani?"

Don't ask me if I'm okay. Please.

"I'll be out in a minute," I choked out in between heaves. Alcohol burns on the way up also, in case you didn't know that.

"Are you okay?"

Dammit.

"I'll be out in a minute," I said again, more forcefully. It turns out my dad doesn't need to worry about my drinking anymore. Not planning on doing it again soon.

When I was sure I was empty, or at least kind of sure, I rinsed my mouth. As much as I wanted to brush my teeth, Sara told me long ago to never brush my teeth right after puking. Something to do with acid. So I rinsed and rinsed and used a little mouthwash. You know, in case we started kissing.

Cole was waiting for me in the breakroom and looked relieved when I appeared.

"Did you get sick?"

"Do we have to talk about it?"

"No. Just wondering. How do you feel?"

"Better. But my head hurts. And my mouth is so dry."

"Do you have a sports drink or anything here?"

"Sara has tablets she adds to water on gym days." I found the container on a shelf and handed it to him. "Would this work?"

"Perfect. Do you have some water?"

I drank the fizzy orange concoction carefully, a little at a time, because there was no way I wanted to puke again with Cole here.

He sat at the table and watched me sip, his eyes dark and intense. That made me feel self-conscious, and I completely forgot how to drink like a normal human being. Orange-flavored electrolytes ran down my chin, down my neck, and into my bra.

"Oh man, you're a mess." Cole started laughing and handed me some napkins.

"I am a mess," I cried, and laughed. "Sorry."

"Why are you sorry? I was the one who got you drunk."

"That's true. But Cute Joint Guy got me high."

"You thought he was cute? He was a douchebag."

"Yes, but he was nice to me." I hiccupped again. "I can't believe I'm still drunk."

"You're high too, don't forget."

"Am I still high? I thought I was just drunk." Then I started giggling and no matter what I did, I couldn't stop.

"That would be a yes." Cole smiled. "Drink more water. I need to sober you up before you go home."

I was suddenly feeling very warm, so I stripped off the snowman sweater before beads of sweat could start rolling down my face. Cole watched me intently, which didn't help my warm feeling. The T-shirt I wore underneath was tight, and I looked like a cat burglar dressed in black from head to toe.

Cole grabbed my hand, pulled me from my chair, and pulled me onto his lap.

"You look very sexy right now, Dani. Any risk of more puking?"

I didn't know I was going to puke just a few minutes ago until it was halfway out.

"I don't think so?"

His right hand snaked around my neck, and he pulled my face down to his. His kiss was soft and sweet at first, not even as sexy as the one under the mistletoe. But it still made my toes curl. His kiss deepened, and when his tongue touched my lips, nudging them apart, I almost slid off his lap. The kiss was delicious, and my hips were gyrating against his lap. His lap responded accordingly.

Don't do this, Dani.

The voice in my head needed to shut up.

Just as Cole's hand left the back of my neck and began traveling towards my boob, Kat walked in and started growling while giving Cole the death stare.

"That cat freaks me out." Cole nuzzled those words into my neck.

"I think she's trying to warn me against you."

"She can go jump off a cliff." The nuzzling tickled.

"Let me put her back in the bathroom." I climbed off his lap and picked her up. This didn't make Kat happy, and she glared at me and growled again. "I'm sorry, Kat. I just want some time with him. When he's not afraid you'll rip him to shreds."

Cole stood and welcomed me back with another kiss and immediately grabbed my boob. I melted into his arms and didn't stop him when he pulled my shirt up and my bra down.

From the bathroom, Kat started making sounds no cat has ever made before. Screams. Like a fox in the wild. Like a woman screaming. The sound broke through my reverie, and I stopped Cole's hand before it could reach between my legs.

"Cole. Wait…"

Kat stopped screaming.

Cole waited. His hand was still on my abdomen, but he had stopped heading downward.

"I'll stop if you want me to, but I think you want me to keep going. Deep down you want this, don't you?" He nuzzled my neck. "Let me make you feel good."

The screaming from the bathroom started again.

My head was spinning. I didn't want to be half drunk and high my first time having sex, and I definitely didn't want it to be here, in the breakroom of Charms & Chapters.

"Cole, stop."

He stopped, stood, and pulled away, shaking his head. Then he immediately started unzipping his jeans. "You got me so hard I need to jerk off or I'm going to be in pain."

"You can't jerk off here! We drink coffee here!"

"Blow me?" He pursed those luscious lips at me.

This isn't happening. All of a sudden I felt completely sober, despite being queasy and having a headache, and I guessed this was what a hangover felt like.

"I guess I'll go back to the party if you don't want to do that. You sure you don't want to?" He sounded hopeful.

"I'm sure. It's not that I don't want to, but not when I'm drunk and not here where I work with my stepmother!"

"Well, you sound pretty sober right now, and I have a mattress reserved at Lorelei's—you know, so I didn't have to drive." He ran his finger down the center seam of my leggings, starting at my belly button and stopping just below the waistband of my underwear. "Come with me."

"You want me to go back to the same party I wanted to leave just a little while ago?"

"I need you. Don't make me go back there like this without you."

He needs *me*, or just relief? Cole was supposed to be my hero but he was turning into Cole the bad boy. Why this surprised me, I'll never know. Isn't that exactly what I wanted? I was not having any of this though, and the longer it went on, the more used I felt.

"I'm not going back with you. I'm sure one of those other girls will be eager to help you."

"C'mon, stop. Don't be like that. I like you, Dani, so maybe another time?" He whispered in my ear, "I need more of what I just had."

That made my entire body erupt in goosebumps.

"Yes." I didn't expect to say that. I wasn't sure I even meant it.

But Cole took the invitation and ran with it. He pulled me close and began to explore my mouth with another kiss. My lower half grew hot and liquidy, and I could feel a second heartbeat in a place that was not in my chest. I briefly considered going back to the party and sleeping with Cole. He wasn't the only one with an unmet need. But soon sanity and a ripping headache prevailed. I reluctantly pulled back and sent him on his way.

I peeked out the window to watch him walk down the sidewalk back to Lorelei's. I wondered if one of the other women he had kissed under the roving mistletoe would help him out of his... situation.

A pang of jealousy tinged with regret came over me. I know Lorelei would be all over him, and he might not even need the mattress he had reserved.

"I got him primed for you," I said wryly.

I needed to freshen up and clean up the bathroom. It was almost midnight, and I still had to face Dad and Sara and lie about what a delightful time the party was.

And thank the Universe, the damn cat had finally stopped screaming.

CHAPTER 26

SARA

Erik and I were both sound asleep sitting up on the couch when Dani came home just after midnight. The TV had gone on playing episode after episode by itself.

"You're home!" I said with a yawn.

Erik was still snoring. That man can sleep through an earthquake.

"I'm home!" Dani said, a little too brightly for my taste.

"Hey! We were worried about you. You okay? We heard about Tristan."

"I'm okay. Can we talk about this tomorrow? I really need to pee and take a shower."

Dani was upstairs in a flash, leaving before I got any good dirt from her. I wondered if she and Cole had spent much time together at the party. She looked a bit ragged, but I couldn't quite get a read on her.

I rubbed Erik's arm to wake him up.

"Mmmmm. What time is it?"

"After midnight, baby. Dani's home. We can go to bed."

"What happened with Tristan? Do you know anything?"

"Nope. She said she had to pee and shower and ran upstairs."

"She hiding something?"

"I couldn't tell. She was in front of me for all of about fifteen seconds."

Erik's face was concerned. "I'm going to go talk to her."

"She's in the shower now. Maybe you should wait until morning."

"I can wait as long as I need to."

CHAPTER 27

DANI

I stood under the hot water in the shower for a long time, trying to wash the night away. I wished I could wash my brain as well. Shame bubbled in my stomach and for a minute I thought I was about to puke again. The headache wouldn't quit. Maybe I was just hungry. I thought about going back downstairs to raid the refrigerator, but I remembered I had some nuts on my nightstand. They're just a bag of pistachios I keep in my room in case I need a snack. Sara asked me once why and I told her they were my emotional support nuts, which made her laugh, so the name stuck.

It felt so good to climb into bed, clean and comfortable, safe and sound. While my body was tired, I doubted my brain would let me get much sleep, so I started scrolling TikTok on my tablet and munching pistachios. I wondered how long a hangover was supposed to last. My head still hurt and brushing my teeth didn't help the taste in my mouth. Checking online, I found the answer: 8 to 24 hours. My stomach lurched thinking about this going on all day tomorrow. Or it might have been the pistachios.

I heard a soft knock on my door.

"You okay, kiddo?"

"I don't feel so good, Daddy."

The door opened and I saw my dad's worried face.

"Do you want to talk about it?"

I hiccuped and sniffed. "Tomorrow?"

"Sounds like a plan. Get some sleep."

After the door closed I started to cry and continued until my body couldn't produce any more tears. I sipped some water and blew my nose at least eleven times before I calmed down. I never wanted to feel like this again. This totally sucked. The entire night played out over and over in my head like a reel on repeat. The shots. Cole. Cute Joint Guy. Cole. More shots. Coughing up smoke. Doorbell guys. Cole. Kissing Cole. Twinkle lights. Things got fuzzy then. I'm not entirely sure how I got from the party to the bookshop. But I vividly remembered what happened with Cole when we got there. The flu-like feeling hit me just from thinking about where and how he had touched me, and I debated running to the bathroom. Swallowing down the urge, I gave my nose one last blow, flicked off my light, and closed my eyes.

Tomorrow morning was going to suck for so many reasons.

CHAPTER 28

SARA

When Erik came into the bedroom, he looked like he was going to burst out crying. I've seen him tear up dozens of times, but outright cry? Not yet, but I had a feeling I was going to soon.

Once he managed to collect himself, I asked the critical question. "Was she drunk?"

"I think so, and from the looks of it she's already hungover."

"Dammit. I'm sorry, baby. I'm disappointed and I'm sure you are, too."

"We had some expectations, didn't we?"

"And we all know what happens when you have an expectation."

"Yup." Erik paused and looked at me. "I mean, what can I even say to her? Other than she's not twenty-one yet, but obviously that didn't cross her mind tonight."

"That's a start. Maybe she learned her lesson."

"I feel guilty cheering on the hangover, but she needs to feel like crap right now."

"The crappier the better, right?"

Dani's morning was going to suck for so many reasons.

CHAPTER 29

DANI

I slept a lot better than expected, but now my head felt like it was swollen and filled with cotton and my eyes hurt from crying. After going to the bathroom and brushing my teeth, I squared my shoulders and went downstairs to face the music. It was already 10:00 a.m., and I was so grateful I didn't have to open today. That also meant Sara wouldn't be here, which meant that conversation wouldn't happen at the same time as Dad's. I would be blessed with hearing how badly I screwed up twice.

I smelled bacon and my stomach growled, overriding my dread of a lecture.

"Hey," I said to my father's back, and sat down at the table.

"Hey yourself." He waved a spatula at me. "Eggs and bacon coming right up."

He put a tall glass of something green in front of me.

"Dad, I don't know if I can drink that."

"Try. This, coffee, greasy eggs, and bacon are the trick. You feel pretty shitty?"

"I feel pretty shitty."

"Good."

"Dad, just get it over with, please."

"What? A lecture?"

"Yes, a lecture." I tried to roll my eyes, but they hurt to move, so I stopped. It was also very bright in this kitchen. Was it always this bright in here?

"Do I need to? Do I need to tell you that you're still underage? That Lorelei could have gotten in a lot of trouble if you had driven somewhere and caused an accident? That alcoholism runs in our family? That you may not be able to start and stop drinking whenever you want? Casual drinking may not be an option."

His voice was smooth and calm but deadly serious.

"Dad, I know. And I promise I'll never, ever do that again. This is horrible."

It was more horrible than he knew, but there was no reason to bring Cole into the conversation.

"What happened? What made you decide to drink? How many were there anyway, just out of curiosity?"

"Four drinks." I mean, why lie? No sense downplaying it. "Something fruity with a coconut taste."

"Ah. Sounds like a punch that actually punched. Well done. If you're going to do it, do it right."

"I'm done with alcohol. Just thinking about it makes me feel sick."

"Drink the green stuff. It really will help."

"I hope so. Did you tell Sara? I don't care if you did but just tell me."

"I did. She was disappointed, but you know how Sara is. I'm sure she'll need some one-on-one time with you. Plus, we need to hear what happened with Tristan."

"I know. Tristan broke up with me last night over the phone while I was walking to the party. I felt really sorry for myself, and I kept thinking 'why not,' which was not the right thing to do."

I chugged the green drink to minimize the time it would be in my mouth and followed it with a mouthful of coffee. "Thanks for just being a dad and not going all AA on me."

"You're welcome." He slid two greasy over easy eggs onto my plate, added some bacon, and buttered some toast for me. He kissed the top of my head lightly, and my tears spilled over.

"I love you, Daddy."

"I love you too, kiddo."

CHAPTER 30

SARA

T his was the first of the two Sundays before Christmas, and while I expected Charms & Chapters to be busy, I was unprepared for the amount of customers out shopping. I had to take at least two names and numbers for people who needed gift wrapping but requested Dani only. I tried not to take this personally. It's not like I don't know my limitations, but I still hated being reminded of them daily.

I promised to call them when—or maybe I should say *if*—Dani came in. I had heard nothing from either her or Erik, and I hoped their conversation went well.

Probably because I was a little on edge, I kept darting glances at the front door every time I heard it open. At one of those tinkles I was surprised to see Cole to walk through the door, dressed in jeans and looking a little worse for the wear himself.

"Hi, Cole. What brings you in on a Sunday?" I was assuming it was to see Dani, and I was right.

"Is Dani here? I just wanted to make sure she got home okay last night."

"No, she's not in yet. I expect her soon though. Were you at the party?"

"I was."

He wasn't very forthcoming, so I motioned him into the breakroom.

"Look. We know Dani was drinking. She was as sick as a dog. What do you know about that?"

Cole looked down at his hands, his feet, the table, anything except directly at me.

"I swear I didn't know she wasn't used to drinking."

"Not used to drinking? What did you expect? She's nineteen, Cole. She's underage."

"I feel terrible. Honest. I just wanted to make sure she's okay today."

I know he didn't literally open her mouth and pour alcohol down her throat, so I took my anger down a notch. Before I could continue, Kat strolled in and started growling. Dani followed the cat through the curtain and stopped short when she saw Cole standing there next to me.

"Hey," she said.

"Hey," he said. "You okay?"

"Yeah. I'm okay."

The bell rang near the register, meaning a customer needed assistance, and both Dani and Cole looked at me expectantly. I could take a hint, so I went out to manage the sale.

A few minutes later, both appeared from the back room, Dani looking a bit smudged, Cole looking smug.

"I'll see you tomorrow," Cole said. "Bye, Sara."

"Bye, Cole." I gave him a pointed look, Kat hissed, and Dani stared at his departing back like a puppy.

❧

It was late afternoon before the shop slowed down enough for me to actually talk to my bonus daughter.

"Let's make some coffee and talk."

Dani looked up from dusting. "I knew this was coming."

"What kind of stepmother would I be if it weren't coming?"

After pouring mugs for each of us, I checked the shop before waving Dani to sit with me at the table. We'd hear the shop door tinkle if anyone came in.

"How do you feel?" I figured I'd start out slowly.

"Much better." Dani fiddled with a rip in her jeans, her eyes filling with tears. "I don't know why I did what I did. Tristan broke up with me and I just had the fuck-its."

"Oh, the fuck-its. I am familiar with them."

"I got really drunk, and I puked. A lot."

"At the party?"

"No. Here. I came here to sober up before going home."

I nodded, but I had to ask. "Alone?"

Dani hesitated. "No."

"Cole?"

"Yes."

These one-word questions and answers were going to take all night.

"Are you guys together?"

Dani looked up from her jeans. "Maybe? I don't know. We made out last night and he kissed me just now in the back room. But he hasn't asked me out on a date or anything."

"Well, he came over today just to check on you, so that's a good sign."

"Don't give him too much credit. He slept at Lorelei's last night. So he didn't have far to go."

"Fair enough."

"He kissed a lot of girls last night, not just me."

Finally Dani was opening up and talking about details. "Mistletoe?" I guessed.

"Yeah. Lorelei was holding it over different girls, and Cole was kissing them. Like really kissing. With tongue."

"I can see why you might be confused."

"He kissed me first. I thought it was real, and I was on cloud nine. And then I heard someone say 'okay, my turn' and I opened my eyes to see him moving on to the next girl."

"I'm sorry, that had to suck."

"Yeah. And then I started feeling sick, so I left and came here. Cole came with me because I was not walking too well."

I suspected there were a lot of details she had left unsaid. Maybe someday she would share them all with me. I just hoped she'd heed the warnings from the cards, her own body, even Kat, and do the right thing with Cole.

Kat jumped up on the table and looked at Dani, prompting her to speak again.

"Oh, I just remembered something. Last night when Cole and I were kissing in here, Kat was acting all kinds of strange. I put her in the bathroom because I was afraid she would attack him. She started screaming. Actually screaming. But when we stopped kissing, she would stop. How could she possibly know?"

Kat hopped into Dani's lap and stared directly into her eyes.

"This cat is freaking me out," Dani said. "Maybe you were right when you said it's Lily."

Kat started purring, rubbed her head against Dani's neck, and jumped down to eat.

I watched Dani watching Kat. Her face looked tired and drawn and a little green.

"How about you go home and get some sleep? You look like you could use it. I'll take names and numbers for gift wrapping orders."

I really needed to up my wrapping game. Maybe next year.

CHAPTER 31

DANI

I was not expecting to see Cole in the breakroom with Sara, and I was very glad the register bell rang so that she was called out of the room and we could be alone.

"You sure you feel okay this morning?" Cole asked.

"Better. My dad made me this disgusting green shake that he said would knock any hangover out, and he was right. I feel pretty normal right now."

"I was worried about you."

I looked up into Cole's eyes, and I did see worry there. Something else as well. His hand reached around the back of my neck, and he kissed me. Long. Deep. A makeup-smudging type of kiss. This guy should give lessons.

He hadn't shaved today, and his stubble burned my cheeks and chin, so I guess I'd have red cheeks for the next few hours. This kiss was worth it. I desperately wanted to ask him if we were together or if he was just having some fun. My body was tingling again from his touch, and I momentarily regretted not sleeping with him last night. I tried to imagine what it would be like to wake up next to him every morning. I smiled against his mouth, and Cole broke the kiss to see what I was smiling at.

"What?" he asked, his eyes hooded and staring at my mouth.

"Nothing. Just you. You make me smile."

Cole booped me on the nose with his finger. "You're adorable. I need to run some errands before I go home, so I'll see you tomorrow, okay?"

We walked out of the breakroom together, and Sara watched us closely. Kat gave a loud hiss, startling one of our customers who sat near her bed.

"I'll see you tomorrow. Bye, Sara."

I realized Cole and I hadn't even exchanged cell numbers. Or asked each other's last names. Was I just a mistletoe kiss? He wouldn't have come in today if that was the only thing I meant to him. I'd already spent a lot of my time convincing myself he was interested and the other times convincing myself he was not.

Tristan was still blowing up my phone from the night before, so I sent him a text telling him I was fine and to please stop worrying about me. I was so tired of people asking if I was okay. I was not okay, not really, but I was okay, if that made any sense.

Everything in my life was haywire except for my dad and Sara. And Charms. And the dogs and Kat. But the rest of it… Oof. Haywire. I don't know what I want to be when I grow up; I don't have a boyfriend, or maybe I have a new boyfriend. I'm just getting over a hangover. I disappointed Dad and Sara, and that green shake this morning has been reminding me all day that I drank it. Shitshow may be too strong a word, but haywire fits.

When Sara told me to go home early, I followed her orders. The streets were busy with shoppers and cheerful faces. Festive decorations and colorful lights filled the shop windows all along the street. It was hard not to feel happy looking at all this, but I was doing a pretty good job of it. The mopes were hitting as I got closer to home, and I just wanted to get in my jammies and curl up in bed hugging Molly.

My dad was cooking dinner when I came in and he looked up in surprise. "You're home early. Feel okay?"

"Yes, Dad. I'm okay." I had to put forth an effort not to roll my eyes at his question. "That green stuff though, I keep burping it up. Is that normal?"

"It's been a long time since I needed to drink one, but yes, I seem to remember lots of burping. Is it helping though?"

"Yeah. I'm going to go upstairs and lie down for a while." I looked at his dinner prep and noticed it included homemade french fries. My stomach growled so loudly he heard it and laughed.

"Go on. I'll yell when the french fries are ready."

"Thanks, Daddy."

"You're welcome, kiddo. I'm glad you're okay."

I'm not okay, but I will be. And then people can stop asking me. I could hear Sara in my head. *We ask because we love you.*

Sometimes I wish she'd stay out of my brain. Not all the time. Just sometimes.

My french fries were delicious. Nice and salty, just how I love them. Almost as good as Hot Dog Johnny's are.

"Are you going to eat anything else for dinner except french fries?" Sara asked.

"Maybe. I'm going by what my stomach accepts and rejects. Right now, it's accepting the french fries and then I'll wait before adding anything else in."

"Convenient, considering it's your favorite food," Sara said with a smile. "You have four orders to wrap tomorrow if you're up to it."

We're open seven days a week until the 23rd, though we may open for a few hours on Christmas Eve. Normally we were closed on Monday and Tuesday, but this season has been so busy we've kept normal hours even on those days.

"I'll go in a little earlier tomorrow morning and whip them out before we open."

Sara smiled her thanks and went back to her dinner as I cleared my plate. Apparently, my stomach was only accepting french fries tonight.

I found Molly on her back, still sleeping on my bed where I'd left her to go downstairs for dinner. I rubbed her offered belly.

"Not hungry, girl? Dinner is happening."

The word "dinner" broke through her nap, and she trotted downstairs to join Tank looking for handouts. We don't call him King of the First Floor for nothing. He always gets the first treat. Always.

I climbed back in bed and curled up on the warm spot Molly left. Tristan was on my mind, and I realized that the pain I was feeling about our relationship was from the hit to my ego that he broke up with me before I could break up with him. I wasn't heart-broken. It was one thing in my life I wasn't unsure of. Tristan was not "the one." I grabbed my pillow, hugging it to my chest, and let myself drift off, but my sleep was uneasy and filled with unsettling dreams of Cole and Tristan.

CHAPTER 32

SARA

Erik was the first one up on Monday morning and surprised me in bed with my favorite mug filled with delicious steaming bean liquid.

I sat up and took the mug from his hands. "Thank you, baby."

"So let me get things straight in my head, see if I have it right so far." Erik tapped his temple. "Tristan broke up with Dani. Dani is okay with that. Dani likes Cole. Cole helped Dani get drunk, so we're not happy with Cole, and we don't know if they are dating. Is that it so far?"

"Yes." I yawned and sipped my coffee. "But don't quote me because my brain is not awake yet."

Erik leaned over and kissed my forehead. "Can I wake it up?"

"You can try. But you'll stand a better chance if you let me drink this." I raised my mug in salute.

"I am nothing if not patient."

And that was true. Erik was even-tempered and self-aware; those two traits made him the perfect partner for me. I swallowed the rest of my coffee, put the mug on my nightstand, and pulled my soon-to-be husband on top of me.

I then whispered the sexiest words ever into his ear: "Dani's opening."

～

Before leaving for Charms, I checked in with my best friends, the Cell, and brought them up to date on the Dani situation. Luckily, we seemed to have crises at different times, so there were always at least two out of the three able to talk each other off the ledge. If it weren't for them, wedding details would have pushed me into the fetal position by now. At least the dress was perfect. Dani would do my hair. I would do my makeup.

I was still musing about footwear when I walked past Lorelei's gallery. It was dark, the sign flipped to Closed. Her windows were large and there was a dim light coming from a room off the main gallery. Lorelei was standing in the doorway, her back to me. I paused to watch her, feeling like a voyeur yet not letting that stop me. I saw another arm appear, and the hand gripped the back of her neck and pulled her into the room and out of my sight. Looked like Lorelei was getting some action. Good for her. She was young, talented, and gorgeous and should enjoy her gifts.

Cole's delivery truck was parked on the street, and I half expected to see him when I walked into Charms & Chapters, but it was just a handful of customers and Dani. She waved at me from the wrapping area, and I waved back, gesturing at her to give me a minute to get coffee.

Just as I came out of the breakroom with my mug, Cole walked in with a delivery.

"There you are," I said. "You must have been in your truck when I walked by."

Cole gave me a strange look. "Yeah, probably."

He waved at Dani and left before she had a chance to pause her wrapping and talk to him. Her face fell, and she went back to cutting sparkly ribbons.

~

As soon as we had a lull in shoppers, I asked Dani if she was ready to talk about what happened with Tristan.

"I guess."

"Let's go to the breakroom. Drink cawfee and tawk." I was a Jersey girl through and through, so that's what I sounded like, even when I wasn't trying to make Dani smile. I was aware. My out-of-state friends liked to get me to say all the words that make them laugh.

"So how do you feel about Tristan? Do you feel better now?"

"I guess," Dani said again. "I'm not heartbroken. And now I don't have to feel that pit of shame when I'm thinking about Cole. Although just thinking about Cole makes me feel strange."

Kat meowed from her litter box.

We both looked down, and she was staring at us from the entranceway to her box. She meowed again and returned to her business.

"Maybe it's your gut trying to tell you something."

"My guts have been telling me lots of shit for the past thirty-six hours. I can't pinpoint one thing."

I had to laugh. This poor kid has been through a lot between boy trouble and feeling like crap physically. I've had a couple of hangovers in my life, and they are not fun. I don't drink at all now, mostly out of respect for Erik. Alcohol doesn't need to live in our home or to be on my breath when kissing my fiancé. I don't miss it, and besides, between Erik and Ethan, I'm familiar with what alcohol can do to a life.

"I'm glad at least one thing is off your plate. You don't have to have that conversation now. You're free to pursue Cole, or anyone you want." I'm not Team Cole, but I didn't want to shut Dani down if she needed to talk to me about him. Talking shit about him to her and telling her to stay away from him wouldn't work. It's her relationship. But that didn't mean I wasn't keeping a very sharp eye on it. I may have been the first of us to admire his shape, but now he was one big walking red flag to me.

So yeah. I'm watching.

CHAPTER 33

DANI

I met Sara's eyes across the table. I knew she didn't like Cole. She didn't have to say anything. And usually I'd listen to her and her instincts, but Cole had some weird hold on me. My entire body reacted to him. I wanted to explore Cole in lots of different ways, and I shivered and got goosebumps. Then a little nausea. I started feeling warm and grabbed a napkin to wave in my face.

"Hang on," Sara said, and whipped out her pink fan that looked like a vibrator.

The breeze felt awesome, and I stopped caring what it looked like. "Thanks."

"Were you just thinking about Cole?"

How does she know this stuff? "Yes. And yes, I felt a little sick, but it passed."

"And this happens every time?"

"Pretty much," I admitted. "But then it passes and I'm fine."

Sara tapped her chin. "This sounds familiar. But I don't know why."

"I texted Tristan finally today to let him know I was okay."

"Heard anything since?"

"Nope."

"I wonder if he'll still come to the wedding with Lisa and Rachel," Sara mused.

"I hope not! That could be really awkward."

"I'll text them later and just ask," Sara offered.

"Okay, thanks. If he doesn't come, can I invite Cole?" I watched Sara's face fall.

"Dani... I hate disappointing you, but I would really prefer a Cole-free wedding day."

"You're just mad at him for giving me drinks. He's a nice guy."

"A nice guy doesn't feed alcohol to a nineteen-year-old and get her drunk." Sara's voice was deadly serious. "And that sick feeling? That's your body telling you something is not right. Listen to it."

She was aggravating me and I was done with this conversation, so I finished my coffee and stood. "I get it. You don't like him. But I do."

"I'll back off. But I am serious about not wanting Cole at my wedding, and I guarantee your father would say the same thing." She paused. "Probably worse, now that I think about it."

"Fine, I won't ask him." I left Sara sitting at the table and went back to my wrapping station to catch up on the holiday requests. I hated it when Sara and I were at odds, and it didn't happen often. But if I'm going to date Cole, she needs to accept him and trust me.

The next few days were tense at home. We were polite, but there was a wall up on Sara's side and I admit there was one on my side, too. By Friday, though, feelings were healing, and we fell back into our normal routine.

Cole came in every day with a delivery, and once, when Sara wasn't around, we snuck into the breakroom to kiss.

"Thinking about me?" he asked after kissing me.

"Yes. Are you thinking about me?" I gazed up into his beautiful face.

"Of course I am." He slipped a hand behind my head, holding the back of my neck and kissing me even more deeply. When he pulled back, he said, "I have to get back to my route. I'll see you tomorrow, baby."

"Cole?" He paused at the curtain. "Do you want my number so we can text or something? I don't even know your last name. And you don't know mine."

"Sure. Let's do that tomorrow. I really need to get going."

Kat strolled through the doorway, right past Cole's feet. She gave him her best side-eye and hissed at him as she walked by.

"That cat freaks me out," he said as he left.

The bell rang at the register, and I went back to work with an uneasy feeling. I realized it was Friday. I wouldn't see him tomorrow.

And he was already gone.

CHAPTER 34

SARA

I was glad when Dani and I got back to normal, and we spent Friday evening shoe shopping and finishing our Christmas shopping. We were loaded down with bags after a hugely successful trip and walking back to my '67 Beetle when my phone started blowing up with Cell mail. I always know something is happening if more than three emails come in in short order. That means either a Cell 911 or a back-and-forth between Lisa and Barb, and God forbid I miss anything.

"Do you mind driving? I have a couple of emails I need to read."

Dani loves to drive the Bug and had picked up driving a standard shift quickly after her father and I started dating. During the winter months in Lavallette, the streets were deserted, and Route 35 was wide open. We could practice starting and stopping without worrying about traffic. Teaching her how to shift on the hills of northern New Jersey was a little trickier, but she had finally mastered not stalling out.

"I don't mind!" Dani grabbed the keys from my hand.

We loaded the bags in the back, and I opened the email thread to see what was happening. The two of them had me laughing in no time. They were planning to throw me a bachelorette party/wedding shower. My online scrapbooking girlfriends were even going to attend via some link Lisa was providing everyone with. The theme was male genitalia because for some reason these women thought I was obsessed with beenises. That's right. Beenis. It's what I preferred to call it. That story goes back many years, to my early days at the dental office.

A new patient had called, and he spoke with a heavy accent. I had some difficulty understanding him, but he slowly explained in stilted English that his three-year-old son had a pain in his mouth and wouldn't stop crying. I checked with the doctor and then told the dad to bring him right in. I just needed to get the child's name to put on the chart and schedule.

Me: What is your son's first name?

Father: Penis.

Me: Penis?

Father: Yes. Penis.

Now, I know I'm hearing him wrong, but I must put him on hold because c'mon. Penis? I compose myself and continue.

Me: Can you spell that for me, please?

Father: B-E-E-N-I-S.

Me: Oh! Beenis.

Father: Yes. Beenis.

So, I make a chart, and I write little Beenis's name on the schedule in the operatory.

Ten minutes later, dad walks in with the cutest little boy, who has obviously been crying. I hand the paperwork to dad to fill out, and when he hands it back, I see the correct spelling of Beenis's name.

It was Dennis. Not Penis. Not Beenis. *Dennis.*

But that would now and forever be known as a beenis, not a penis.

The Cell warned me that more than a few beenis-related gifts would soon start to arrive, and where they should be delivered, home or Charms & Chapters? It was always safer to use the bookshop at this time of year, since it felt like we lived there.

Dani was pulling in the driveway when I finally got done chatting with Lisa and Barb. I warned her what was coming.

Pun intended.

CHAPTER 35

DANI

Monday morning dawned early, and I groaned when my alarm went off. We had just had the busiest weekend in Charms & Chapters history, and both Sara and I were exhausted last night when we finally got home. Dad and Sara pulled the age card and voted for me to open the shop in the morning. Christmas is two days away and today is our last full day of being open. Sara is thinking about working tomorrow, if just for a few hours in the morning for last-minute shoppers. But we still needed to get through today.

Verity was waiting at the door when I arrived. She appeared in my sight line just after I left the house, which meant she had been waiting a while.

"Dani! Thank goodness. It's freezing."

"Good morning, Verity. You're a little early."

"I was walking from a different location, and I didn't calculate my arrival time very well."

"How long have you been out here?" I asked incredulously.

"About a half hour, give or take a few minutes."

"Oh, Verity, come in! Let's get you warm." I unlocked the door and waved her inside. "I'll put a pot of coffee on and kick up the heat."

"Thanks, Dani. I just need a few more gifts for people."

"You must have a huge list of family and friends. I have wrapped like a dozen for you already."

Verity blushed and looked down at her feet. "Yes. I'm very blessed."

I wondered about that. Verity was always alone and walked everywhere. I'd never seen her with another person.

I smiled. "I'm happy for you."

Verity went to sit down in her favorite seat to warm up and wait for her coffee. Kat got out of her bed, stretched, and did her best parkour over to Verity's chair. Then she did something very un-Kat-like. She curled up in the woman's lap, closed her eyes, and started purring. Verity and I met each other's eyes, clearly equally shocked. She'd been around Kat long enough to understand that this was an unusual occurrence, but I could tell it touched Verity's heart to be the recipient of Kat's attention.

She patted Kat and scratched her ears just like the cat liked. Kat pushed her head against Verity's hand and bobbled her nose when Verity bent her head to kiss the top of Kat's.

"Do you have any pets, Verity?"

"No, dear. I used to have a cat many years ago, but she's been gone a long time."

"I'm sorry. Let me go start the coffee. I'll be back soon. Just relax and warm up."

"Kat is helping me. She's like a little heater in my lap."

I flushed, thinking that Cole gives me a little heater in my lap. I hoped he'd be in soon so we could finally exchange numbers and last names.

I made a pot of coffee and delivered a mug sweetened with a touch of sugar to Verity, still happily enjoying the kitty in her lap. It was time to raise the shade and flip the sign to Open.

I was busy checking out a customer at the register when Cole came in with a delivery.

He waved and dropped the box near me. "Hey, Merry Christmas in case I don't see you tomorrow."

"Wait, Cole, hang on." I finished the transaction, thanked the customer, and turned towards him. "Hey. I was hoping we could talk before Christmas."

"I'm kind of slammed right now, Dani. I'll try to stop by later."

"Maybe around closing time?" Except I wasn't closing. But I could stay anyway.

"No promises, but I'll try, okay?"

That didn't sit right, but what was I supposed to do? Kat woke up from her new bed, a.k.a. Verity's lap. She didn't jump down, but she kept her gaze on Cole, and I could hear low growls emanating from her throat. It didn't seem to bother Verity though, so I turned my attention back to him. I tried to play it as cool as he was playing it.

"Sure. Whatever." I was feeling a little used and, again, a little nauseated. He kept giving me mixed signals. I was already tiring of never knowing if Cole was going to be warm and horny or cool and businesslike. I mean, I realize he's working, and it's almost Christmas so he's busy, but he still doesn't have my phone number. I let a guy feel me up, try to go farther, claim he was hot for me, and yet he doesn't have my number. And I still don't know his last name.

Sara came in finally and took over the register to give me a break.

"I'm loving the business we're doing, but I'm looking forward to less busy days," she whispered.

"Yeah, I agree."

"Crap." Sara shuffled around under the counter. "We just ran out of register tape. Would you run over to Lorelei's and borrow a roll? I know she has the same terminal we do."

"Sure."

I was glad to step out and get some fresh air. There was snow in our forecast for tomorrow, and you could smell it.

I noticed Cole's delivery truck parked in front of the gallery, but when I entered, there was no sign of him. Or Lorelei for that matter. I stood there looking around for a minute.

Lorelei's disembodied voice came through the speakers. "Hi, I'll be right down. Hang on."

I noticed the cameras focused on the door. Must be motion-activated, so Lorelei could go upstairs to her apartment if she needed something without missing a customer or risking theft.

Voices and footsteps were coming down the internal staircase into the gallery.

"Hey, sorry about that. I just had to run upstairs for a minute."

Lorelei seemed ruffled. Her red lipstick wasn't immaculate, like it normally was. Her braids were wild and her dress looked strange. And not strange in her usual funky, artistic way. As she got closer, I realized her dress was inside out.

I had a very sick feeling. And I wasn't just suspicious. I knew I was right. Cole was here. He was upstairs with Lorelei and her dress was inside out because she wasn't wearing it while with him. She had let him do what I wouldn't. Not that she shouldn't. It wasn't like we were exclusive or anything. But she knew I liked him, so this felt pretty shitty. Merry freaking Christmas to me.

"Sorry to interrupt you guys." Sarcasm seeped into my voice. I couldn't help it. "Can we borrow a roll of register tape? We just ran out."

"Interrupt what? I just needed something upstairs."

Cole chose that perfect moment to come down the stairs into the gallery, and Lorelei had the good grace to blush and look at the floor.

161

"Dani, I'm sorry," she said. "Can we talk about this later?"

I looked at Cole and wondered what happened to the guy who had saved my butt on the ice. The guy who carried me over the threshold with a hurt ankle. How did I ever picture us together? He was just out for a good time, with anyone who would allow it. My stomach turned.

"Neither of you owes me any explanation. Have fun with each other." I grabbed the roll of paper Lorelei had in her hand, burst out crying, and ran out of the gallery.

I stood outside just out of view of the Charms & Chapters window, composing myself. I hated crying. It's just that when I feel frustrated, I cry. My heart was feeling bruised from being hurt twice in one week. And right before Christmas! First I was dumped by a decent guy who I didn't even love. Then I got used by a horny guy who just wanted to hook up. When I wouldn't do it, he found someone who would, just as I expected. It sucked that it was Lorelei, though. Every time he delivered there, I would imagine him delivering his own package to her. This was going to suck. I was going to have to see him nearly every day at work. At least I didn't have to see Tristan regularly. Small blessings.

I wiped my eyes with my sleeve and pulled open the shop door. Sara was banishing some dust bunnies and looked up with a smile, which faded instantly. I guess I was doing a shitty job hiding my feelings.

"Do you want to talk about whatever just happened?" Sara took the roll of paper from me and replaced the empty spool.

I burst out crying again and ran into the breakroom, collapsing at the table. Ego blows hurt. I was sad. I was ashamed. Everyone in the store saw me crying just now. And to top it off, I'm single at Christmas with no hope of getting a boyfriend within the next twenty-four hours.

Sara parted the curtain. "Can I come in, or do you want some time by yourself?"

I shrugged my shoulders. "You can come in, but I don't want to talk about it yet. I'm just crying non-stop and don't even know why."

"It's your body releasing something that hurts. Never be afraid to cry something out. It's a great equalizer."

Kat came into the breakroom and jumped in my lap, rubbing her head on my chin.

"Even Kat knows something bad happened. Let me know when you're ready to talk." Sara rubbed my back. "And if you want to go home, go. I can manage the next few hours."

Her kindness made me cry harder. "Okay, thanks. I might. Once I stop crying."

If I ever stop crying.

CHAPTER 36

SARA

Seeing Dani crying like her heart was shattering into a million pieces broke my own heart. I wondered what Cole had done. It had to be Cole. No one else would have that big an impact on her. Plus, it's Christmas. And Tristan just broke up with her. Topping it off, she just got over her first hangover. It would have been a lot to handle for anyone.

Dani wiped her eyes and blew her nose. "I'm okay. I just... I found out that Lorelei and Cole are together."

"Oh, no... But I thought you and Cole had something brewing." The electricity between them was obvious.

"Not anymore. And now I am going to have to see him every day."

"So you caught them together? Is that how you found out?"

"Yeah. It was horrible. And I just knew before I was even sure."

I remembered yesterday's voyeur moment when I saw Lorelei being pulled into a room. That must have been Cole. I felt my anger ramp up.

"I'm disappointed that Lorelei would do that when you guys talked about you liking Cole."

"Cole is interested in one thing and one thing only. She just let him have it." Dani started crying again.

"You know what this is? This is a perfect example of Rule Number One," I said.

Dani sniffed. "What's Rule Number One?"

"Boys are stupid."

That made her smile. "Is there a Rule Number Two?"

"Oh yes. There are lots of rules. Once you factor Rule Number One into your life though, it will explain a lot."

"So, what's Rule Number Two?"

"Sometimes girls are stupid, too. But it's almost always because of Rule Number One."

Dani snorted. "I think this is actually both Rule Number One and Rule Number Two in action."

"You have a point."

"I feel a little better. At least I don't feel like I'm going to burst out crying anymore. Thanks, Sara. I'll be okay. Give me a minute to freshen up and I'll get back to work."

"Take your time."

The register bell rang, so I left her sitting there and went out to the shop. Verity was waiting there with another dozen boxes of incense.

"Is Dani still here? Can she wrap?"

There is no way I'm going through this again next year. I'll take lessons if need be. I'm an artist. How hard can gift wrapping honestly be?

"Yes, Verity, Dani is in the back. She'll be right out. Would you like some more coffee while you wait?"

"Oh, that would be lovely, dear. Thank you."

By my count Verity had bought at least ten books, twenty boxes of incense, and a dozen crystals so far. Everything Christmas giftwrapped. How did she have that many people to give gifts to when she's always alone, walking around town or here at Charms? I had a feeling that Verity was more complicated than I thought.

165

After getting her settled, I poured her a mug of coffee and let Dani know there was a wrapping job awaiting her attention.

"Does it ever get any easier, Sara?"

"Does what get easier? Work? Boys? Life?"

Dani groaned. "All of the above."

"There are times in life when things run smoothly. Enjoy those times because they can change on a dime. You're getting hit from all sides right now, and I know how unsettling that can be. Life goals, Tristan, Cole, the hangover, the holidays, your mom not being back, the incredibly busy days we've had here. It's a lot."

Dani nodded. "Yeah. It feels like a lot."

I pulled Dani to her feet and gave her a hug. "You'll get through all of it. I promise. I must deliver this to Verity, and you have boxes to wrap. Let's revisit this when we have more time."

Dani seemed to perk up as she expertly wrapped Verity's incense and topped each one with a coordinating bow. She brought them up to the register and I carefully put them in the reusable tote Verity had brought with her.

"All ready, Verity!" I called out to her.

Gently, Verity lifted Kat off her lap and placed her in the bed on the windowsill.

"Thank you, dear. Are you open tomorrow?"

"I haven't decided, to be honest. It's supposed to snow, and I didn't advertise I'd be open so I'm leaning towards not. Were you thinking of doing more shopping tomorrow?"

"Oh no, tomorrow is a busy day for me. Very busy. No shopping for me. I wanted to bring you a small offering. For always being so kind to me." She touched my hand. "There are some days where you and Dani, Molly, and Kat are all I see. I meant to bring it today, but my brain didn't catch up to my feet earlier, and I left it at home."

"That's so nice, Verity! Thank you. I can't wait to find out what it is. We'll have limited hours in the week between Christmas and New Year's. I might not be in much, because I'll be getting things ready for my wedding on New Year's Day."

"I'm so happy for you, Sara. Erik is such a nice man. And so handsome. You know I have all his books in hardcover. Will he do a signing here when his Belvidere book comes out?"

I smiled. "I'm pretty sure I could talk him into that."

"Have a blessed Yule, Sara."

"Blessed Yule to you, Verity."

"Dad just called in a Thai order and we're going to pick it up when we close, which is in 3... 2... 1. Closed." I flipped the sign, locked the door, and pulled the shade.

"We made it," Dani said. "This was our busiest season yet."

"It was definitely a successful couple of months."

"Where is the cat carrier?" Dani asked.

We always bring Kat home during the holidays. It's one thing to leave her overnight here at Charms, but if it's going to be any longer than that, we always bring her to the house.

"Bathroom closet."

"At least we don't have to bring the litter box back and forth."

"I agree. That's a thankless job."

She had a similar setup at the house and her own bed both in our room and in Dani's. Molly didn't seem to mind sharing her space, and Tank rarely saw Kat. She stayed upstairs most of the time, whereas he was restricted to the first floor by virtue of his short legs.

We picked up our dinner and walked home together, Kat yowling in the carrier the entire way. I can't imagine what our neighbors think.

Not that I care. What other people think of me is none of my business.

Some Erik wisdom from the rooms of AA.

CHAPTER 37

DANI

I woke up on Christmas Eve morning with Kat sitting on my chest, staring at me. Last night when we got home, Sara had tried to put her in their bedroom and Kat screamed and ran out the door, down the hall, and into my room. She refused to leave my side, even joining us at the dinner table, sitting at my feet while we enjoyed our Thai food. I didn't know what had gotten into her. After dinner, Sara moved the litter box into my room.

"There's really nowhere else to put this?"

"I always have it in my room since she usually sleeps there. So now you get the honors."

As if on cue, Kat entered the box for her nightly visitation.

"Dammit, Sara!"

My soon-to-be stepmother just laughed and wished me good night. As for Kat, she was sitting there in her box, making it harder to breathe by the minute, gazing at me.

"Merry Christmas Eve, Kat," I whispered.

Kat bobbled my nose and rubbed the top of her head on my chin.

"Are you a magical kitty? Sara says you are. She thinks you're Lily from the shore." Kat kept staring at me, so I continued. "But if you are Lily, can you just tell me, please? It won't freak me out any more than I already am."

The stare went unbroken, and Kat gently put her paw on my cheek, claws retracted—thankfully. She blinked slowly and let out a small meow.

"Was that a yes?"

Another meow.

Maybe Sara wasn't as off base as I originally thought.

Sara made blueberry pancakes for breakfast and had a feast planned for our Christmas Eve dinner.

"Rouladen, mashed potatoes, red cabbage, and string beans. A good German Christmas Eve dinner. Doesn't that sound delicious?"

Sara doesn't spend a lot of time in the kitchen, so Dad and I were crossing our fingers that this meal would be as successful as Sara imagined.

Her pancakes were pretty yummy, so hopefully that was a positive indicator for tonight.

It started snowing right before lunch and it came down quickly, coating everything. I was grateful we didn't need to go anywhere in the next couple of days.

Kat was asleep on her bed, and I was just about to start streaming some mindless reality show when Sara knocked on my door.

"Can I come in?"

"Of course."

Sara sat on the edge of my bed and rubbed my arm. "How do you feel today? Now that you've had time to wake up and eat, do you feel better about what happened yesterday?"

Honestly, I was burned out on the topic of Cole, but Sara wouldn't let it rest until she knew I was feeling better.

"I guess. It just sucks that I'm going to see him all the time. The whole thing just sucks." I felt like I might cry again now that I said that out loud.

"Don't forget you're going to get a few days break from seeing him. Maybe by the time we reopen the shop it won't be as big a thing as it is now."

"And maybe Santa will bring me a boyfriend for Christmas." There was more than a hint of sarcasm in my voice.

"Maybe he will. There's magic all around us. Especially right now." Sara stood to leave. "Keep your options open. You never know when doors might open."

The doorbell rang at the exact moment Sara said those words. She grinned at me. Molly and Tank started barking, and Erik was yelling at them to get out of the way. It was unusual for someone to come to the front door, so Sara and I peeked around the corner to look downstairs. My dad opened the door and a man with a familiar face stood there, smiling ear to ear.

I heard Sara gasp, and she tore downstairs squealing, "Ethan! Holy crap, you're here!"

She grabbed him and pulled him inside, allowing me to see the two people behind him.

"And you must be Diana. Welcome, sister-in-law! And Jace, my new nephew. Please come in, come in! I didn't know you'd be here before Christmas. This is amazing!"

"I wanted to surprise you. We got the chance to move our tickets up and took the leap. Thankfully, the hotel could accommodate the added days."

My uncle Ethan was very handsome. He looked like a male

version of Sara, and his smile was as striking as his sister's. His new wife was also attractive, and she gazed at her husband in adoration as he talked.

And then I saw Jace. Cute was an understatement. Blond hair, tan, surfer-dude look. Sara introduced everyone to my dad and then looked around, apparently realizing I hadn't followed her downstairs.

"Dani, come down. My family is here!" Sara sounded practically giddy.

I ran back into my room and checked myself out in the mirror. I wasn't planning on seeing anyone but Dad and Sara today, so I never went further than brushing my teeth. My hair was a mess, and I still had my pajamas on, but at least my breath was fresh. A quick brush through my hair and rubbing the sleep from my eyes had to be enough. Besides, even though this cute guy was standing in my living room now, he lived in Australia. After the wedding, I'd probably never see him again. Certainly not boyfriend material, although Santa sure had come through with some eye candy!

I held the railing on the way downstairs so that my first impression wasn't a klutzy one.

Jace turned to watch me, and his face lit up. *I* made his face light up. That was a good sign. I heard Sara introduce me to everyone, but my eyes stayed on Jace. Jace the Australian hottie. I murmured polite *hellonicetomeetyous* at my new uncle and aunt but immediately brought my gaze back to his beautiful blue-green eyes. The color of the sea in the tropics. His hair the color of sand and his skin, as far as I could see given his winter coat, deliciously tan. I wondered what it would taste like on my tongue.

Merry Christmas to me. Cole who?

CHAPTER 38

SARA

Seeing my brother for the first time in years took my breath away, and it was the best Christmas present I could have hoped for. Ethan looked great, healthy and beaming with happiness. His beautiful wife glowed with the same energy, and I had such warm feelings at the intensity of their love. Considering how hard it was for Ethan to have hit his bottom, seeing him so happy made *me* so happy. And I knew how he felt. I suspected that his and Diana's were the same intense feelings that Erik and I shared.

I turned around, particularly excited to introduce Dani to Diana's son, Jace. She wasn't behind me, as I had expected. "Dani, come down. My family is here!"

Jace was adorable. With his blond hair and tan, he looked like he stepped off the set of Baywatch. Maybe he'd help Dani move on from Cole. And Tristan, for that matter. Kat came to the top of the stairs to see what all the commotion was about and then joined us in the living room to rub everyone's ankles in one of the most social interactions I'd ever seen from her. She sat at Jace's feet and gazed up at him with questioning eyes until he squatted down and scratched her behind the ears. There was no hissing, no growling, no spitting. Just head butts and purring.

Dani skipped down the stairs, and when she saw her soon-to-be step-step-cousin-by-marriage, I could tell all thoughts of Cole had flown out of her head. Another Christmas miracle.

"We don't all have to stand right here all afternoon. Let's get comfortable. Are you hungry? What would you like to drink?" My questions were rapid-fire partly because of excitement, but also probably linked to the entire pot of coffee I'd already finished today.

I got everyone settled and comfortable in the living room while Erik took drink orders.

I patted Ethan's arm. "It's good to see you looking so wonderful. I'm so proud of you, Ethan."

"Thank you. I feel good. And there's nothing like falling in love in your fifties, right, sis?"

"No argument from me."

Diana spoke up. "Sara, your home is just beautiful. I love all the holiday decorations." She gestured around the room. "You have wonderful taste."

"Thank you! Erik gets all the credit for the outside though, and for braving the death stairs to retrieve the boxes I needed."

Diana's face was quizzical. "Death stairs? Tell me more."

"The stairs leading up to the attic. They're treacherous, and we call them death stairs. I rarely go up, but there is a cool witches' chimney up there."

Diana's eyebrows raised. "Ooh! Can you show me? I just love anything witchy."

"Follow me," Erik offered, walking back in from the kitchen and handing out the drinks he had fixed. "Sara doesn't need to be anywhere near those stairs."

Diana's voice dropped into a conspiratorial whisper. "Is she clumsy like Ethan?"

"Very much so," Erik answered in the same whisper.

Ethan said, "You know we can hear you, right? We're right here." He started laughing. "But I can't say it's not the truth."

When they came back downstairs, Diana couldn't wait to show Ethan the photos she'd taken upstairs.

"Look, love! A real witches' chimney." She turned to the rest of us. "We have witches' marks on the timbers in our attic. Same meaning, keeping the house safe from witches and other evils. Fascinating."

"Very cool." Ethan looked around the room. "Where did Jace go?"

"And Dani?" I added.

"I can answer both questions." Erik pointed towards the kitchen. "They're raiding the refrigerator as we speak."

Diana laughed. "Jace can clean out a refrigerator faster than I can pack it. We should get in there."

Sure enough, the kids already had bread, cold cuts, and mayo lined up on the counter and were giggling as they built sandwiches. It was good to see Dani giggle. Hell, it was good to see her smile.

I leaned over to Diana. "I hope you can come to my bachelorette party next Tuesday evening. It's both in person and virtual for my scrappy girlfriends around the world."

"Scrappy girlfriends?" Diana asked.

"Sorry. I mean scrapbooking. We've been online friends since the early 2000s. My friends Lisa and Barb will be here, and Lisa is setting up a meeting online so they can watch and chime in. Those two are flying in early on Tuesday, one from Michigan, one from Texas."

"I'd love to join! Sounds like fun. Thank you for inviting me. What about the boys?"

"I think he's getting some guys together for a poker game, I'm sure he'd welcome Ethan and Jace."

"Consider them here."

We smiled at each other, already bonding as friends and sisters-in-law. This was going to be the best Christmas ever. I had my family with me, my number one guy, my bonus daughter, and my animals, and my wedding was only a week away.

Diana touched my arm. "You and Erik seem very happy together. How long have you been engaged?"

"Ooh, about 2 years now. We got engaged very soon after we met. When you know, you know, right?" I met her gaze and suspected she knew exactly what I meant. "Life is good, and I'm very grateful for my blessings. My life feels like a storybook romance most of the time. I don't take any of it for granted."

"I understand completely." Diana touched her head to mine. "Is there any food left? I'm starving. And after that, I want to see the rest of this home. I only got a small glimpse when we went up the death stairs, but it looked beautiful."

I peeked around Erik to see if there was anything left to eat on the counter. I was concerned because Dani and Jace were chowing down at the table, with no regard for the rest of us hungry people. Luckily there were plenty of fixings left, and we all stuffed our faces, the rouladen dinner postponed to the following day.

"This is not what I had in mind for Christmas Eve dinner," I said, with a mouthful of PB&J on soft white bread.

The chorus of "It doesn't matter, we love it!" made me feel better. As we all ate, Ethan and I shared stories from our childhood amid plentiful laughter. Before we knew it, darkness fell. Ethan, Diana, and Jace left in their rental car to drive the few blocks back to the quaint Belvidere Hotel, with promises to come back for Christmas morning. The snow was still falling lightly, but the couple of inches on the ground was not impassable. That made me realize how lucky we were to have so much within walking distance here. We had a bit of that in Lavallette, but Belvidere won hands down. Shops, restaurants, pharmacy, a hotel, and some of the most beautiful homes in the county.

Dani trotted past me to go upstairs, and she wiggled her eyebrows at me. "Life just got happy again! Merry Christmas Eve!"

I rolled my eyes and grinned. A Christmas miracle for sure.

CHAPTER 39

DANI

In three weeks, I had had feelings for three different guys. Who does that? Is that even normal? Before meeting Cole, I had lots of feelings for Tristan. Mostly they were about how to break it off with him without hurting him. That's impossible, I realized. Breakups hurt. But before that, I had much nicer feelings for Tristan. Then Cole slid into my life, just like I slid on the ice and into his arms. Cole brought out something completely different in me, something wild and animalistic. I truly believed that. I was ready to have sex with him before knowing his last name or where he lived. He could be married for all I know! And maybe he was. Both Tristan and Cole hurt my ego and self-confidence. I wasn't heartbroken; I was hurt and ashamed.

And then Jace walked through our front door, the exact opposite of Cole yet not the wholesome boy next door like Tristan. Jace is more surfer dude with an edge, which I found out this afternoon after spending more than a few hours with him. Plus, I could listen to Jace talk all day long with his Australian accent. So Tristan and Cole could both go take a long walk off a short pier.

While Jace and I were in the kitchen checking out the food situation, I learned that he's twenty-three and graduated from the University of Tasmania with a bachelor's degree in marine science. This May he'll be working as a paid intern at the Department of Marine and Coastal Sciences at Rutgers here in New Jersey. During the months in between graduation and Rutgers he'd be helping Ethan with some home renovations. When he told me he was coming back, I had goosebumps all over my body and some butterflies, but no flu-like feeling. I took that as a good sign. He'd be here for ten weeks before going back to get his master's degree. Or maybe he'd like to stay in New Jersey and get his master's here.

"Have you always known what you wanted to be?" I asked him.

"Ever since I was young. I love anything concerning the ocean. It's an entire ecosystem with mysteries and lessons to be discovered. As a kid my mom always had trouble getting me out of the waves."

"Maybe you're a merman deep down inside."

"Maybe." Jace smiled. "I love to scuba dive. Have you ever done that?"

"No, but I've snorkeled. Does that count?"

Jace laughed. "Kind of. Would you like to learn to scuba?"

With Jace? I'd be happy to learn anything he wanted to teach me.

"Absolutely. It must be so quiet and peaceful."

"Actually, it's not as silent as you'd think. There's the exhaled air and bubbles from the regulators for one thing. And the sea creatures make noise. Whales, dolphins, even shrimp."

"Shrimp make sounds?" That was something I'd never thought about.

"Yup. They make clicking, popping sounds. So do crabs."

"And you can hear that underwater?"

"You can hear it, but sometimes it's hard to tell what direction the noise is coming from."

"Do sharks make noise?" Sharks were one of my biggest worries whenever I was in the ocean. "Or do they just sneak up and bite you?"

"Some do. Sharks are fascinating." Jace chuckled at the look on my face.

"Fascinating? I'd use a different word, but you do you."

With his background, no wonder he was so tan. It was summer in Tasmania, and he spent a lot of his time outside. When he spoke about his wish to be an oceanographer, his eyes lit up and his words quickened, making it harder to understand him but more exciting to listen. He was passionate about his career choice, a certainty that once again made me feel adrift. I haven't wanted to be anything specific since I was a little girl. My interests and passions changed so often, I couldn't pin down one thing that would fit my wish list.

Although the oceanography thing sounded amazing. The opportunity to put that kind of work into practice with the Jersey shore nearby was tempting. It would mean at the bare minimum four years of college though. Was I even ready to commit to that? The career checked off a couple of my boxes, but I didn't want to waste my dad's money if I would not apply myself. That wouldn't be fair, and I loved him too much to do that to him. Plus, was it oceanography that sounded so amazing, or was it Jace that sounded so amazing?

He was so easy to talk to. There were no awkward silences. I told him all about my life, about working at Charms & Chapters, how I just wasn't feeling the pull in any direction towards what I wanted to be when I grew up. He told me about life in Australia and what an oceanographer's daily life might look like. He's looking forward to doing field work this summer at Rutgers.

"What do you do for field work?"

"Take water samples, do reef surveys and fish counts, stuff like that. From what I know, other people can even do a ride along and help."

My ears started to tingle, and I knew Sara would say it was the universe telling me to listen.

"Maybe I could ride along with you sometime?"

"I'd like that."

"Yeah, me too."

The whole conversation with Jace about his education had me wanting her to do another tarot reading with oceanography (and Jace) as my focus. The last one had absolutely nailed my situation. And it spoke of a healing relationship… Could that be Jace?

After he and his mom and stepdad left, I spent the rest of Christmas Eve doing internet research about oceanography and cursing myself for not asking Jace's last name.

When I finally decided it was late and time to call it quits, I shut down my tablet and plugged my phone in. I turned off my lamp and looked out my bedroom window to see the snow still lightly falling. The footprints Ethan, Diana, and Jace left getting to their car had been well covered in the few hours since they left.

A white Christmas. That could only mean good luck. Jace would be here at least a week, and he'd be back in the summer. That was so exciting. I pictured riding along on field work with him, Jace showing me what his future looked like, maybe even what *our* future looked like. My brain jumped ahead to the random thought that our babies would probably have blond hair.

My phone vibrated with an incoming text.

> **JACE**
>
> Hey Dani, it's Jace. Ethan got your number from Sara for me, so I hope it's ok. Wanted to say thanks for the great talks and I'm looking forward to many more. If you're still awake, Merry Christmas, it's midnight.

> **DANI**
>
> I'm awake! Merry Christmas. Yeah, it was a great day. I'll see you in a few hours!

There were no visions of sugarplums dancing in my head, just gentle blue-green oceans and Jace's blue-green eyes blending into one another as I dozed off.

~

I awoke to the smell of bacon and the sound of Molly galloping downstairs. After hitting the bathroom, I decided to forgo a hairbrush, a toothbrush, and a robe and ran downstairs to get my fair share of bacon. I skidded into the kitchen in my fuzzy socks yodeling "Merry Christmas," when I noticed Dad and Sara were not alone in there.

My face must have gone as red as the Santa hat on Uncle Ethan's head, but then everyone yodeled "Merry Christmas" back at me and we all laughed. Suddenly I caught Jace's gaze and remembered what I looked like. And probably smelled like.

"Be right back." I backed out of the kitchen, grabbing a piece of bacon off the counter before running upstairs to make myself presentable. A quick shower with some berry-scented body wash (no time to wash hair), a brush of my teeth, a little mascara and some concealer on the zit that Santa kindly left for me, a brush through my hair and a messy bun, cute red loungewear with candy cane socks, and I declared myself ready. I did all that in less than ten minutes. A new world record.

I sauntered into the kitchen this time. "Let's try this again. Merry Christmas, everyone!"

"Merry Christmas, Dani!" came the response from everyone except our three fur babies. Molly was sporting a red and green ribbon tied to her collars, and she did grin at me. Sara made both dogs wear ribbons on Christmas morning. Molly didn't care; goldens are mellow like that. But Tank hated the ribbon, and it generally only lasted a few minutes before he was scratching at it and Sara took it off. She tries it every holiday. And fails miserably every holiday. This time seemed no different, as his was no longer tied to his collar and he looked properly grumpy despite the bacon he likely had already begged for. Sara told me she tried to put one on Kat's collar and the cat simply refused, as they do.

I walked around the table hugging first Dad, then Sara, before moving on to my soon-to-be aunt and uncle. When I reached Jace, he stood, depositing Kat from his lap onto his mother's, and gave me a proper hug like a good step-step-cousin-by-marriage should.

"Merry Christmas, Dani. I didn't know I was coming on this trip until the last minute, so I don't have gifts for you—for any of you."

"Join the club. I didn't know you even existed until Sara got Uncle Ethan's email this month. So you're forgiven."

"Next Christmas will be better. More notice. And maybe you'll come to Australia to celebrate."

"Maybe." I smiled and gazed into his amazing eyes.

Diana clapped her hands. "What a splendid idea! It will be warm, no snow, but we will do it up beautifully. Absolutely join us next year."

My mind was already calculating how much time Jace and I would spend together, and the full body zings started again. It was so amazing to not feel queasy like I did when I thought of Cole. Just anticipation. And Kat liked him. That was a huge plus. That he lived a world away sucked, but what's a twenty-hour flight between step-step-cousins-by-marriage?

"We could make that work. I could set my next book in Australia…" Erik's voice trailed off as his muse hit him with ideas and his brain left the kitchen.

"Who needs more bacon?" Sara asked with an amused glance towards her fiancé. "I think I've just inherited the job. And Australia for Christmas sounds lovely. We'll have to figure out what to do about the animals and the shop, but that's not impossible."

Jace met my eyes and grinned while Sara's words rang in my ears.

That's not impossible.

CHAPTER 40

SARA

I felt a bit of déjà vu as I watched the smiles and looks exchanged between Dani and Jace. It reminded me of when she and Tristan first met on the beach and couldn't take their eyes off each other, grinning like fools the entire time. Thankfully, the energy between Dani and Jace differed from her energy with Cole. That was more explosive and sharper edged, where this was warm and gentle, though the attraction was undeniable. Jace and Cole couldn't have been more different from what I could see, but judging from Dani's face, she was not thinking about Cole at all.

I watched my husband-to-be as he struggled to stay in the conversation, his mind clearly already orchestrating his next novel in Australia, before turning to my brother. "Ethan, I volunteered you and Jace to help Erik move the furniture out of this room on New Year's morning, if that's okay."

"Yeah, sure. Absolutely." He turned to eye Jace and Dani. "That's okay with you, Jace, right?"

No response.

"Jace?" he repeated.

Nothing.

"Hey Jace, Santa just landed in the front yard."

Jace tore his eyes from Dani's and looked at his stepfather. "Mate. He's supposed to come down the chimney. And, like, hours ago."

"Did you hear me ask you about moving furniture?"

"I did not. But I will. What should I move and where?"

"Not now," I said. "New Year's morning."

"Of course, Aunt Sara. I'll be happy to help."

Jace flashed a dazzling smile at me and turned his attention back to Dani, who hadn't taken her eyes off him. I'm pretty sure her heart felt better, and I marveled at how perfectly timed all this was. Once again, the Universe oversaw everything beautifully. Now, if we could just keep that happening until the wedding was over, I'd be eternally grateful.

Ethan caught my eye and pointed at the kids, rolling his eyes. I snorted in a most unladylike way and a sip of coffee caught in my throat. I coughed until tears rolled down my face. The thought popped into my head that as much as I love coffee, chocolate never did me like that.

A buzz from Erik's watch shook him from his thoughts. "I promised to make the coffee for the 11:00 a.m. men's meeting at the church annex. The guy who was supposed to do it this month is away with family. What do you say, Ethan? Want to go with me?"

"Yeah, absolutely. Let me get my boots back on. We're taking your SUV, I assume?"

"Yes, we're taking the SUV because it's a tank, goes through anything. I'm not sure how well plowed we'll be this morning, but at least it has stopped snowing for the moment." Erik looked at me. "You guys okay to wait on opening presents until we get back?"

"Go!" I said. "Enjoy the meeting. Diana and I are going to discuss wedding details until she wants to choke me."

He said, "Dani?"

Dani seemed to be struggling not to roll her eyes. "I don't care,

Dad. I think Jace and I are going to walk around town and look at the lights."

"The ladies have spoken," Erik announced. "Let's go, Ethan."

～

After cleaning up the kitchen from the breakfast mess, I started prepping the rouladen we were supposed to have eaten yesterday. Prepping was honestly too strong of a word. All I had to do was brown them. Erik would make the gravy. Dani's specialty is her delicious mashed potatoes.

"What is rouladen?" Diana asked. "They look delicious, but I've not heard of them."

"It's very German. Thinly sliced beef, spread with mustard, wrapped around a mixture of dill pickles, onion, and bacon, browned and simmered in brown gravy for hours."

"I know I just ate a huge breakfast, but that made my stomach growl. Sounds delicious!" Diana rubbed her hands together in anticipation.

"Ethan probably hasn't eaten it in a long time. We grew up on this for Christmas Eve dinner. He liked it back then, so hopefully he still does."

～

The rouladen was simmering nicely in the electric skillet when Erik and Ethan returned from their meeting.

"Perfect timing. I need you to make the gravy."

"Oh man, that smells amazing," Ethan exclaimed. "I haven't had rouladen since I can't remember when!"

"I was hoping you still liked it." I smiled at my brother. "It's nice that we are sharing this again."

"Life is good. Finally. There have been too many years of it being a struggle just to get through the day."

"I'm so proud of you, Ethan. Proud of my fiancé, too." I pulled Erik into a hug. "Best Christmas ever. Now please go do the gravy so we can open presents!"

We all sat in the living room and Ethan played Santa. Given that he was still wearing the Santa hat, it seemed only fitting.

"Listen—since we left home sooner than expected, we didn't have time to get you guys anything for Christmas." Ethan paused. "But Diana and I put our heads together and we have an offer for you folks. Sara, you told me a while ago that you weren't planning a honeymoon because of the shop and animals, but last night you said it wouldn't be impossible to come to Australia. We want you to come visit, Dani too. And we don't want to wait for next Christmas. Diana's nephew owns a spectacular five-star resort near our home in Queensland on the Gold Coast. It would be our treat for a couple of weeks. It's beautiful in January. What do you think?"

Erik and I looked at each other. Was this a no-brainer? Abso-freaking-lutely.

"We'd love to!" we said in unison.

Ethan gave Diana a high five. "That didn't take any arm twisting. What a delight!"

I started making lists in my head of everything I'd need to arrange for us to spend two weeks in Australia. *This is not impossible.* I'm going to repeat that as a mantra until things are in place. Normally Dani would be here to cover the shop and the pets, but there was no way she would turn down an opportunity to come with us and see Jace. And by the look on her face, I knew I was right.

187

Erik, Dani, and I exchanged small gag gifts. We donated the bulk of our holiday purchases to a local children's toy drive. Erik gave me a box of the urinal cake incense, Dani gave me a certificate good for ten gift-wrapping lessons, and I contributed a snore guard nose thing for Erik and earplugs for Dani. I'm pretty sure our neighbors could hear us laughing. That made me wonder how much they really hear on a daily basis. Maybe I should have gotten earplugs for the surrounding homes, too.

I poured the rest of the coffee into my mug and put on a fresh pot for everyone else.

"Does anyone want to take a Christmas stroll to walk off breakfast? I'd love to show you the shop."

Diana jumped to her feet and pulled Ethan up from his chair. "Sounds delightful."

"How were the roads, babe?" I asked Erik. "Any issues?"

"Not really. The sidewalks aren't done yet though, so be careful."

Dani looked up in alarm. "You're not going on the walk with them, Dad?"

"I'm going to stay here and monitor the rouladen and shovel our sidewalk."

Jace and Dani kept their faces neutral, but I could read Dani like a book. She met my gaze and rolled her eyes at me. I winked and shrugged my shoulders. She'd get plenty of alone time with Jace this week.

"I'll shovel for you, Uncle Erik." The "uncle" came out of Jace's mouth so smoothly that I gave him some extra props, not that he needed any.

"Yeah? That would be much appreciated, Jace. The shovels are on the porch by the front door."

Ethan, Diana, and I headed out for the shop, Ethan carrying a shovel so that we could get inside. The ground was covered with easily five inches of fresh snow, giving us a true white Christmas. Most of the sidewalks were already clear, but every so often we had to cross into the street, the three of us holding on to each other so we wouldn't fall. Each home along the way was lit with Christmas lights, and it was breathtakingly beautiful against the snow. The windows of the apartments above all the shops were softly glowing, Christmas trees lit, and you could easily imagine what this picturesque town looked like back in the 1800s when candles were used to light the trees and the streetlights.

When we got to Charms & Chapters, Ethan shoveled the sidewalk and the short entranceway to our front door.

I unlocked the door and ushered them into the shop.

"Oh, Sara! This is just lovely." Diana's eyes swept over the shop. "It's perfectly boho yet Victorian all at the same time. Ooh, those chairs look comfortable."

Diana wandered around, gently touching the crystals and smelling the boxes of incense. "Sara, what scent was the incense Erik gave you? You both got quite a laugh from that."

"Urinal cake."

"I'm sorry, what?"

"Urinal cake."

Diana stared at me with her mouth hanging open and a box of incense in her hand, apparently forgotten.

I waited as she processed my words.

She slowly asked, "Why do you sell urinal cake incense? Why do they even *make* urinal cake incense?"

"Oh, it wasn't exactly marketed as such. The local vendor we use had some sort of production error and I determined for myself that it was urinal cake scented."

"How do you know that, sis?" Ethan had taken notice of our conversation.

"Why does everybody ask me that?"

"Well, I mean, think about it. You're a girl. You go into the ladies' room. There are no urinal cakes in there. So logically that means you've been in a men's room." Ethan *tsk*ed. "What were you doing in the men's room?"

"How do you not know this? Ladies' room equals a long, slow line. Men's room equals quick in and out with a guard at the door." I *tsk*ed back at him. "Keep up."

Ethan put his hands up, laughing. "I give. Ready to walk back? I hear the rouladen calling my name. Is it safe in Erik's hands?"

"Very safe. More than in my hands, for sure."

"That's comforting, sis."

As we left the shop, I noticed Verity walking towards the bar down the street, making her way cautiously around uncleared areas, her arms loaded with bags, some of them clearly filled with familiar wrapped packages. I realized that her "family" must be her bar family. That made me feel better, knowing she wasn't truly alone and would be with people she cared about today.

"Merry Christmas, Verity!" I called out to her, my voice carrying easily through the quiet afternoon, with all sound dampened by the snow.

"Merry Christmas, Sara! You aren't open, are you?"

"No, just showing my family the shop."

"Well, have a wonderful holiday." And with a wave she turned and continued her trek to the bar, which was all shoveled out and had its Open sign blinking in the window.

Funny how some people in my life needed a meeting on Christmas, and some needed a bar. Both were fellowships.

CHAPTER 41

DANI

I wanted to maximize the time I had with Jace, so I grabbed a shovel and just stayed out of his way while still trying to appear to be helping. He made quick work out of the sidewalks and cleared the fire hydrant at Dad's request.

"Snowman?" I asked him, throwing a loosely held-together snowball at him.

"Wow. Pretty poor excuse for a snowball."

I stuck my tongue out at him. "Snow's too dry for a snowman anyway. Won't pack."

"Any other great ideas?"

"Snow angels?" I flopped down onto my back and waved my arms and legs along the ground.

Jace hit the ground next to me but didn't leave enough room for any waving on his part. He propped himself up on one elbow and leaned over me. "You make a beautiful snow angel, Dani."

"Thank you, kind sir."

His eyes locked on mine, and I could not believe how warm I was, considering I was laying in five inches of snow.

Maybe I should kiss him, I thought.

So I did.

Two seconds into the kiss, I heard my father knocking at the window. Jeez! We barely got time to start! I turned my head towards the house and my dad just smiled and waved and made the "I've got eyes on you" motion with his fingers.

I really needed to find my own place.

During dinner, we talked about the upcoming trip to Australia, settled on our dates in January, and volunteered Sara to book the flights. The amount of time we'd be spending on a plane sucked, but Jace was the pot of gold at the end of the rainbow.

After dinner, Sara's family—and soon to be my family—went back to the hotel after lots of hugs and kisses and claps on the back. Sara and Dad made themselves comfortable on the couch, turned on some Christmas music, and sipped hot chocolate.

"Have you decided when you're going to open Charms & Chapters this week?" I asked Sara.

"I'm not sure how much traffic we'll get, but I guess we should open some and test the waters. Last year, the week between Christmas and New Year's was dead, remember?"

"So tomorrow maybe?" My stomach pitched a little at the thought of seeing Cole, but I pushed him out of my brain and focused my thoughts on Jace. And maybe Jace would like to visit me at the shop, where my dad could not make his "eyes on you" fingers at me.

"Do you want to work for a few hours?" Sara asked.

"I could do that. I'll just get bored sitting around here. How about I open at 10:00 and close at 2:00 if it's quiet?"

"I'll leave that totally up to you. Don't forget to update our social media whatever you decide to do. And maybe take Kat with you for a change of scenery."

I texted Jace about my plans for the next day and tried to sound nonchalant when I said I'd be alone at the shop for a few hours. You know, just in case he might want to stop by and kiss me. Or something.

Now what to wear? Maybe the low-cut jeans and a bodysuit. I'd skip a big breakfast so my stomach would be nice and flat. Sara always laughed at me when I complained about my huge stomach. She always threatened to show me what a belly really looked like. Sara often wished aloud that her gym work would flatten it, but like Dad said, she's soft and squishy in all the right places.

I just didn't need to see it.

Outfit prepared, I crawled into bed after moving Kat off my pillow. She's been sleeping there a lot instead of her actual bed. Last night she slept on my head, determined to be on as much of my pillow as she could.

"I'm taking you to work with me tomorrow." Kat stared at me, completely still. "Just for a few hours, then you're coming back here since we may not keep regular hours this week."

The cat blinked once at me and then concentrated on cleaning her front paw. I guessed she was good with that.

I heard Dad and Sara coming up the stairs to go to bed. I called out another good night, and Sara knocked softly and opened the door.

"Jace is pretty cute, huh?"

"Oooh, Jace and Dani sitting in a tree, k-i-s-s-i-n-g," my dad's off-key voice sang from behind Sara.

"I can't with you people." I laughed. "Go to bed. Never mind who I'm kissing in a tree."

Sara winked at me and closed the door. I'm sure she'd already figured out why I was eager to work for her tomorrow. She knew it wasn't to see Cole. That's for sure.

Just as I was dozing off, my phone vibrated. Jace's message was simple.

JACE

See you in the morning.

CHAPTER 42

SARA

"It was a perfect Christmas," Erik murmured in my ear.

"I agree. And I'm so excited about Australia! Lifelong bucket list item."

I was already making to-do lists for the trip, and I was once again so grateful that Barb was managing my wedding details. That let me concentrate on the logistics of all of us going away for two weeks. Closing the shop for vacation was a simple decision. No one else was trained to run it, so we had to close. It's just the three of us and we'd all be away. But taking care of Molly, Tank, and Kat was a different story. Our most precious fur faces could not be left with just anyone. That will require some thinking. Someone staying at the house made the most sense, but trusting the right person was scary.

More murmuring in my ear. "Let's go to bed."

"Did you open your snore thing?" I had given him a robotic-looking device you stick up your nose. It was sort of a joke but also much needed.

"You don't really expect me to wear that, do you?"

"Oh, I expect it. And I refuse to be disappointed."

Erik sighed. "I'll try it tonight just for you. But no promises. It looks like a torture device."

"Good enough. At least try. My earplugs aren't exactly comfortable, you know." I poked his arm. "Tit for tat."

"Tit? Did you say tit?"

"I did. And if you're interested in them, I suggest we go upstairs."

Erik took the stairs two at a time while I let the dogs out, made sure they had fresh water, turned off lights, and double-checked that the doors were locked. I found him in bed with the puffy duvet pulled up to his neck.

"What took you so long?" he growled. "I'm freezing. I need your body heat."

"I'll be with you shortly. Please stand by."

"I'm trying, but please keep in mind that I'm freezing."

"Shrinkage?"

"Maybe?"

"You don't know?"

"Can we not talk about that right now? I just want you in bed next to me. Now."

"Let me wash my face and brush my teeth. I'll be right with you."

"Sara," he groaned. "Hurry."

So I hurried.

Dani was opening the shop, allowing Erik and me to sleep in and have a leisurely breakfast while we waited for Ethan and Diana to come by. We planned on taking them on a sightseeing tour of the area, and Diana desperately wanted to try a hot dog from Johnny's after I had strongly recommended it. I had a feeling Jace would not be with them. I'd bet he was going to Charms & Chapters to keep Dani company. Honestly, it made me feel better that he'd be there if Cole came in. Light versus dark. Both were good-looking, but just like their hair color, one glowed with light and one with darkness.

CHAPTER 43

DANI

Jace arrived at the bookshop shortly after I did, and he both looked and smelled amazing.

"Hey," I said. "Merry Day After Christmas."

"Merry Day After Christmas to you."

I was getting better at deciphering Jace's words through his thick Aussie accent.

"Let me start coffee and feed Kat." I swept my arms out to gesture across the small shop. "It's not big, but it's magical. Have a look around."

"It's really quirky."

It took me a minute to realize he said quirky. It sounded more like crikey, which I know they say in Australia, but I'm not sure if it refers to something good or bad.

I guess my confusion showed on my face, because he kept repeating the word. "Quirky. You know, strange. Odd. Unusual."

"Oh! Quirky. Yes. That's Sara. Her tastes can sometimes be odd."

"Ethan is a little quirky, too. I guess that makes sense, brother and sister and all. He's a good guy, though. I'm glad my mom is with him."

"I am too." He had no idea how much. "I'm excited about going to Australia. It's going to be fun."

"I'm just glad I came along on this trip. I almost didn't, but my mom insisted. Now I'm grateful I did."

"Me too."

We were standing there gazing at each other with silly smiles on our faces when the shop door opened and Cole walked in. Because of course he would.

I was standing close enough to Jace that he must have felt me stiffen.

"You okay?" Jace asked in a low voice.

I could only nod in reply.

"Hey, Dani," Cole said. "Merry Christmas. Listen, I'm sorry about what happened the other day."

He didn't sound sorry.

"Whatever," I said flippantly. "Hope you guys are happy."

Jace stepped between us and stuck his hand out to Cole. "Hey mate. Jace."

"Cole. Are you related to Dani?"

"In a roundabout way, yes." Jace looked at me. "What did we decide? Step-step-cousin-by-marriage?"

"Something like that." I stuck my chin out at Cole. "You have a delivery? Or did you just come in to see if you could try to get in my good graces again? And by good graces I mean my pants."

Cole's face was priceless. For that matter, so was Jace's.

"Listen, Dani. No hard feelings, right? We were both a little drunk. Things got out of control. You know you were just as into it as I was. You could have come back with me. Then Lorelei wouldn't have even happened."

Jace's face went beyond priceless into dumbfounded, but he wasn't going to stay silent. "Are you really saying that to her in front of me?"

"This is none of your business, dude."

"Don't 'dude' me, mate. I think you've been rude to Dani and I'm pretty sure she would like you to leave. I know I do."

Cole put his hands up. "I have no fight with you, man. I just wanted to clear the air with Dani. This doesn't involve you."

"Listen, suckhole, it's the holidays, so I will not let you bugger up my day. Just go."

"What the hell is a suckhole?"

"You. You're a suckhole. Look in the mirror, dipstick."

This was quite entertaining. I could tell Cole didn't understand everything Jace was saying, but he knew he was getting insulted. His handsome face was dark and when he looked at me, his eyes no longer held me in their magic. No butterflies. And no nausea.

Kat came out of the breakroom and started hissing and spitting when she saw Cole.

Jace let out a hoot. "Cats have a good sense of what a person is like. She's got you pegged, mate."

"Whatever. I'm out. I need to stop by the gallery." Cole smirked at me as he said that. "At least someone will be glad to see me."

I made sure the door was shut firmly behind him and watched as he walked down the sidewalk to Lorelei's gallery.

"Good riddance, you asshole." I was no longer feeling anxious about seeing Cole every day. He was not going to be even a blip on my radar. He could drop his damn packages and get out. I had better things to think about.

"I guess he's the guy you told me about."

During one of our long talks on Christmas Eve, I'd told him about Cole and the night we got drunk. I didn't go into great detail, just enough that he could get the drift.

"Yeah. That's Cole. I was worried about seeing him for the first time after all that happened, but it turned into a nothingburger."

"What kind of burger?"

"Nothing. A nothingburger."

"You Americans talk pretty strange, too, you know."

"I have lots to teach you, grasshopper."

Jace's face looked puzzled, but then he shrugged, letting it go. Kat purred loudly and wound around Jace's legs.

"Cats have a good sense of what a person is like." I parroted his words back to him and winked.

I felt my phone vibrating from the pocket of my jeans and checked to make sure it wasn't Sara. When I said goodbye to her this morning, she seemed frazzled even though she'd only just woken up. Probably wedding jitters, but Sara tends to overthink and worry so she may be checking on me in case Cole came in. I couldn't wait to tell her about him and Jace, and how good it felt to look at Cole and only feel a little bruising of my ego. Cole had lost his magical hold over me and I knew Sara would be happy to hear that.

The text was from Lorelei.

> **LORELEI**
> hey I just wanted to say sorry again. i hope we can still be friends

Friends? We were friendly but I wouldn't have considered her my friend. I didn't have a lot of friends, and I think I'd remember if she was one of them.

This time I meant it when I texted back:

> **DANI**
> have fun with each other.

"Everything okay?" Jace asked.

"Yeah. Everything is really good."

He smiled. "Really good."

When he kissed me, it was gentle and sweet and spoke of futures.

CHAPTER 44

SARA

I crawled out of bed after sleeping way too long, dopey with sleep and feeling wedding jitters kicking in. *Perfectly normal,* I said to myself. *A shower will make me feel better.* I stood under the hot water and practiced box breathing, trying not to hyperventilate. After hyperventilating anyway, I let the water hit the back of my neck and shoulders to relax them until I finally felt human again.

I dried off and lotioned my limbs and sat at my dressing table after wrapping myself in the softest, fuzziest bathrobe I own. Dani was watching the shop, and I didn't have anything on my to-do list until this afternoon when Ethan and Diana were coming over.

Staring at my face in the mirror, I slowly picked apart every inch of it. By the time I was done I was depressed as hell. The sun did me no favors. Age spots, according to my dermatologist. And wrinkles. The only wrinkles I loved were my laugh lines. I had laughed more over the past two years than all the decades before and they reminded me daily of how blessed I was. But the rest of them could go jump in a lake.

I lifted my growing jowls with my fingers, which gave me my

chubby cheeks back. The one bright spot was that I now had visible cheekbones. They'd been hidden my entire life.

"What are you doing, babe?"

I dropped my jowls back into place.

"Sara. Answer me."

I picked up my tweezers and clicked them towards his face.

"Just looking for something to pluck, my love."

The look on his face as he backed out of the bedroom was worth it.

CHAPTER 45

DANI

The rest of the days between Christmas and New Year's Eve flew by. The store was slow, so we were closed more than open, which allowed me ample time with Jace. Sometimes we joined the adults with whatever they were doing, but most of the time we hung back at the house and talked. We talked more than I had ever talked to any guy in the history of guys.

Dad and Sara were currently at the airport picking up Lisa and Barb, who would be staying in the room across the hall from me. They scheduled their flights to land within a few minutes of each other, so everyone should be back here by noon, ready to decorate according to Barb's instructions. The bachelorette party was set to go live at 7:00 p.m., both in person and online, and we had been setting up in Sara's studio. It was a shame that the only room in the house suitable for a studio was on the second floor, and I was glad boxes didn't arrive like this every day. Sara had spent more than a few hours there this week trying to get it presentable, but art studios were supposed to be a mess. She worried too much. We've been stacking boxes and bags in there as they arrived at the shop, and the pile was growing noticeably. Since Barb had instructed Sara to leave everything unopened until she arrived, we just had to hope that all was in order and accounted for.

The last thing Sara needed was more stress. She'd been vibrating all week, bouncing off walls, cleaning, and making sure everything would look perfect for tomorrow. I hoped the bachelorette party took her mind off her never-ending to-do list.

My phone announced a text.

MOM

Finally got a flight out of Abu Dhabi
instead of waiting for the cruise ship.
Arriving late tonight and will see you
tomorrow. Happy New Year! Love, Mom.

Sara was going to freaking poop herself.

CHAPTER 46

SARA

Dani was right. I almost did poop myself when I heard her mother was descending on us tomorrow. My wedding day. An occasion that no ex-wife should get near. I could just see Cynthia bouncing in at noon, right as the wedding ceremony started. Fortunately, I was so excited about seeing my two best friends and the upcoming party tonight that I was able to put Cynthia out of my head. For now, anyway.

Barb and Lisa were getting settled into the guestroom, warned by Dani more than once about the thin walls, even though I already had, at her request. I wasn't sure if she was worried about hearing something from the Cell's room or vice versa. Erik carried in their suitcases and more boxes for the night's party from the car.

"How much beenis stuff could exist?" he asked incredulously.

Hoots of laughter from the three of us filled the second floor in response to his question.

"Oh babe, you have no idea how creative these ladies can be. They all started as scrapbookers and can alter the hell out of things."

"I'm just going to stay far out of the way. Us guys are going to play poker in the kitchen. Try to keep the noise down, okay?" Erik tried to make his voice stern. "It's hard to concentrate on the game with a lot of commotion above us."

He failed at his attempt to sound tough, and we all laughed at him. "Us guys" were Erik, Ethan, Jace, Lucas, and two guys from one of Erik's meetings who had no plans for New Year's Eve and could fill out a poker game. The only women coming in person other than the Cell and Dani were my sister-in-law Diana and Lucas's wife Emily. Fifteen of my scrappy girls would be on the video call and Lisa had two laptops set up to strategically show the six of us on camera.

Barb spent a couple of hours on wedding decorations and putting together little favors for each guest so she wouldn't be rushed in the morning. Lisa was helping her and practicing her part of the ceremony, which she had offered to officiate. The house was a mixture of Christmas and wedding, which was quirky enough to make me happy. After the wedding ceremony we were serving several Thai dishes, set to be delivered to the house at 1:00 p.m. Our favorite restaurant wasn't planning on being open on New Year's Day but agreed to make the dishes for the wedding because we were their neighbors and frequent customers. Like, very frequent. Sometimes twice a week. That was what small-town living was like. You took care of each other.

I joined Erik in the kitchen as he set up bowls of snack foods and sodas for the guys.

"Hey, baby... this time tomorrow we'll be an old married couple." I snaked my arms around his waist and tipped my head back for a kiss.

He put his finger up—the one telling me to wait a moment, not the other one. Then he pointed to his mouth and swallowed with some serious miming.

"I have to warn you prior to this kiss that I just had a mouthful of onion dip and garlic potato chips."

"So romantic. Lay one on me anyway."

Boy howdy, did he ever lay one on me. I'm pretty sure my almost-husband is the best kisser on the planet. He also gives the best foot rubs. He's literally the best from head to toe. Pun intended.

I went upstairs to brush my teeth to banish the garlic and onion combo.

"It's time!" Dani met me at my bedroom door on my way back out. "Let's party!"

"Ready for merriment! Where's Lisa and Barb?"

"Already in the studio. Lisa has the whole thing ready. I think most of your girls are dialed in as well."

The Cell had kept me out of the studio until now. I couldn't wait to see the decorations. And they did not disappoint. Crudely drawn beenises were strung from fishing line, hung from every corner over our heads. At our heights, Barb and I were safe from hitting our heads on a beenis, but Lisa and Dani were tall, so it was bound to happen.

Emily and Diana came upstairs together, apparently becoming fast friends on the way to the party.

The girls made me sit in a special chair wrapped completely in beenis paper. They piled the boxes in front of me, and one by one I opened beenis after beenis. There were lots of beenis mugs, a setting of silverware with beenis handles, a gift certificate to an adults-only store a few towns away, a case of lipsticks shaped like beenises, straws with beenis tips, beenis earrings, and more than a few beenis towels.

By the time I was done, we were all laughing until we couldn't breathe, tears rolling down our cheeks. I insisted that Dani collect all the wrapping paper, smoothing them out to save. It wasn't every day you came across beenis wrapping paper. I snickered to myself.

Maybe that's what we would use for my wrapping lessons. Mostly just to mortify Dani.

The girls on the video call started dropping off after a while, but a few hung in while we just chatted about life. We've been through life together—marriages, babies, divorces, sickness, deaths, and everything in between. They are some of my most precious friends and know more about me than most people who live within walking distance. We celebrate our good times, and we cling together in bad. We know each other's husbands' names, babies' birthdays, if we didn't get enough sleep, and what our plans for dinner were. A better bunch of ladies doesn't exist. To me, at least.

"I'm going to run downstairs with all these boxes so Dad can take them out to the garage."

"Good idea, Dani. Although recycling won't go out because of the holiday." I had a feeling the boxes weren't what was drawing her downstairs. I'm pretty sure it was just an excuse to see Jace before he left.

"I'm going to head home," said Emily. "Thank you so much for including me! I'll see you tomorrow! Happy New Year a few hours early." She waved to us as she left the studio and headed next door.

Diana stood up and stretched. "I think I'll check on Ethan. Were you guys going to stay up until midnight?"

"Oh, hell no," I replied. "I need beauty sleep for my wedding day, so I'm going to bed as soon as we're done here!" I yawned. "See? But Erik might. Check with him. You're more than welcome to stay and celebrate here."

"Nope. I am also of the age where beauty sleep is a requirement. The clock striking midnight will find me in dreamland."

Barb and Lisa agreed, since we were all of "that age," and went to the guest room to get ready for bed.

Watching the ball drop on TV appealed to me in my younger days, but now when I watched the NYE festivities all I could think about was where do you go to the bathroom? People crammed together shoulder to shoulder in the freezing cold, listening to singers I've never heard of for hours and hours.

But the bathroom thing was number one in my book of reasons.

～

After I washed my face and brushed my teeth, our bed could not have looked more inviting. I couldn't wait for Erik's game to end and for him to come to bed. I know you're not supposed to sleep together the night before or see each other on the day of your wedding, but we had pooh-poohed that idea. I like to pick which old wives' tales I want to believe.

I was tired but had some butterflies about tomorrow. Guess I wouldn't be normal if I didn't have a bit of wedding jitters rumbling in my belly, even if it wasn't my first time. Dear Universe, please let that be just jitters and not something else. I did not need that adding to my day tomorrow.

I calculated for the fifth time exactly what time I needed to be in the shower to be ready to come down the stairs at noon. There was no way my brain was shutting off tonight. As tired as I was, sleep may be elusive tonight. I needed Erik here to cuddle me and soothe my jittery belly.

As if he had read my mind, and sometimes I thought he did, my soon-to-be husband opened the bedroom door. Erik had a smile on his handsome face and a cup of chamomile tea in his hand.

"I thought maybe this would help you fall asleep."

"How did you know I was having trouble?"

"I can feel you right through the floor. It's that weird magic you have with me."

"It helps that the floors are as thin as the walls. Now please come hold me. I'm feeling very needy."

"Your wish is my command."

Once I was wrapped in Erik's arms, and after I sipped my tea, the rumbles quieted, and I finally drifted off.

At midnight he murmured "Happy New Year" in my ear. At least, that's what he told me the next morning. I was already sound asleep.

CHAPTER 47

DANI

I stopped scrolling my phone to watch the ball drop on TV, wondering if Jace was still awake. Just as that thought crossed my mind, his text came in, wishing me a happy new year. I responded in kind and fell asleep with a smile on my face.

When I finally woke up and went downstairs, I found Sara standing outside the front door in her pajamas, blowing a tiny bit of cinnamon inside the doorway.

"Morning, Dani! It's our big day! I'm just getting my monthly abundance spell done."

Sara followed the tiny cloud of spice inside and gave me a hug, closing the door behind her. "How's my favorite almost bonus daughter this morning?"

"Don't even think I'm going to call you mom after the wedding." I laughed. "I have to draw the line somewhere."

"Funny girl." She stuck out her tongue. "Speaking of mothers, did you get a firmer time from your mom, and please tell me she knows it's our wedding day?"

I had to laugh, especially since she admitted to me why she's so worried about my mom being at her wedding.

"She knows about the wedding. And I'm pretty sure about the time."

"Pretty sure?"

"My mother isn't always good with time. So even if she told me 5:00 p.m., it could really happen anytime. Sometimes early, sometimes later."

Sara gave me a pinched, worried face. "You're sure she doesn't own a gun, right?"

I burst out laughing. "Honest. I told you before. She doesn't have a gun. She knows how to shoot one, but she doesn't own one."

"What about Chris?"

"Honestly, I don't know about him. I've never seen him with one. But I don't spend a lot of time with him."

Sara's face was still pinched.

"Try not to think about my mother. She won't do anything bad. Just be happy your wedding day is finally here!"

Sara agreed, but before we could step away from the foyer, the doorbell rang, so she turned and opened the door.

"Happy New Year, Sara, and happy wedding day!"

"Verity! What a surprise! Thank you."

I peeked around Sara. "Morning, Verity. Happy New Year!"

"Oh, Dani! Same to you. I just wanted to drop off a small wedding gift."

"Come in, please! You didn't have to bring me anything, but I'm so grateful you did."

The older woman stepped inside and handed Sara a package. Sara unwrapped a gorgeous whisk broom decorated with dried flowers and moss, crystals, twigs, and lace. I could see the goosebumps rise on Sara's arms when she held it up.

"Oh, Verity, this is amazing. Thank you so much. Did you make it?"

Verity smiled. "I did, with a little help from my friends."

"Your friends at the bar?" Sara asked.

"Oh no, dear. That's my bar family. Some of the gifts I bought at Charms & Chapters were for them. But twelve went to my special group of women in town."

I waited for Sara to ask about this "special group," but she just smiled knowingly and handed me the broom to admire. Every hair on my arms rose at once.

"This is magical." I showed the older women my goosebumps.

Verity winked at us. "I had a feeling both of you would experience that. If you're ever interested in some group energy like that, just let me know. I'd be happy to welcome both of you."

"Thank you, Verity. For everything. Maybe we'll take you up on that offer sometime."

"You are quite welcome, Sara. May Hecate herself bless your wedding."

When Verity left, Sara and I just looked at each other, a bit dumbfounded.

"So, she's a witch," I mused, "who also likes to hang out at the bar?"

Sara laughed. "I guess they're not mutually exclusive."

"We just learned a lot about Verity."

No wonder Kat loved her. Kindred spirits?

Just as we finished eating breakfast, Jace, Diana and Ethan burst through the kitchen door.

"Happy New Year!" Ethan called out.

Everyone was in the kitchen, dogs and Kat included. Jace looked half asleep, tousled, and adorable. I was really glad I had brushed my teeth before coming down to breakfast.

"Happy New Year again," Jace said to me as he shed his heavy coat. "We walked over since our rental is dodgy in the snow."

It was bone-chilling cold, with light snow forecasted, and his face was rosy from the walk over.

"Happy New Year again yourself. Bacon?" There were still a few strips left near the stove, which both dogs thought would be theirs.

When Jace picked one up and started chewing, both dogs turned their full attention to him.

"You can stare at me all you want. I'm not sharing my bacon."

Molly made her head as round as she could, ears flattened, eyes pleading. It was adorable when she did this. Molly was an expert manipulator, and it didn't take long before Jace succumbed to her magic and shared the rest of his bacon. She walked away chewing happily and Tank took her place, a puddle of drool forming at his feet.

"You are not nearly as cute as Molly, but the drool is gross. Here." Jace broke his second piece of bacon in half and grabbed a paper towel to sop up the drool. He turned to the older men. "Ready to move furniture?"

My dad directed Ethan and Jace into the living room, where the couch, coffee table, and recliner needed to disappear.

"Do you think I need to get Lucas over here to help?" My dad looked worried. "The last thing we need is a muscle pull."

"Isn't he a physical therapist?" Ethan asked. "He might come in handy."

Within minutes Lucas knocked at the door, and the menfolk started moving everything.

"Oh, my." Sara's face blanched. "When was the last time we moved the furniture to clean?"

"Um, never?" I offered. "I'll get the vacuum and duster."

"Thanks, Dani. I need to get into the shower. What time do you want to start my hair?"

"It won't take a super long time, so maybe 11:00 a.m.?"

"Yup." Sara started for the stairs. "After I shower I'm coming back down to cleanse and bless the room, but I'll put my dress on before you start my hair."

It was almost 10:00 already, so I cleaned up the dust bunnies and lit some incense to prepare the room and jumpstart the cleanse for Sara.

Lisa and Barb came downstairs as Sara headed up, and Barb got to work decorating, with Lisa helping. They both shooed me out of the living room, so I cleaned the kitchen and went to shower. When I left the bathroom the smell of burning Palo Santo wood reached my nose, which meant Sara must have cleansed and blessed the living room while I was showering.

I planned to wear a simple long-sleeved sweater dress in silver and black that came almost to my knees, paired with black leggings and Sara's black suede slouch boots. It was perfect. Jace had told me he was wearing black pants with a black and silver sweater. I know what you're thinking. And yes, I took that into consideration when I decided on my outfit. We were going to look fierce together.

I was going to do my hair the same way as Sara, long hippie curls. I wanted to do mine before hers, so I would get a good feel for it. Of course I wanted her hair to look perfect, even though she was far from a bridezilla. She might not freak out over some limp curls, but she'd never forgive me if I burned her hair off. Sara's got some PTSD about that thanks to a time many years ago when a hairdresser burned a half-inch-wide chunk of her bangs off almost to the scalp during highlights. I was going to be very careful not to traumatize her on her wedding day.

I gathered all the supplies I needed to work on our hair and walked down the hallway to Sara and Dad's bedroom. I could hear voices before I knocked on the door.

"Come in!" my dad called out.

I opened the door. "Am I interrupting anything?" You never know with those two.

"No, Sara cut herself and she needs a Band-Aid. Would you look in the medicine cabinet, please?"

Sara was sitting in front of her vanity mirror, still in her robe, holding her head in her hands, her shoulders shaking.

Oh crap, was she crying?

Nope. She was laughing.

"I do not need a Band-Aid. I'm fine."

"Babe. You were bleeding."

"I'm well aware, but a Band-Aid won't work."

"What happened?" I asked innocently.

"You don't want to know."

She was not wrong.

CHAPTER 48

SARA

Dammit. I knew I shouldn't have waited to shave my yeti-like bikini area. I was doing well and only had to change the razor blade once before I cut myself in an area that should never be cut. I definitely knew better than to go there with a normal razor. Waxing? Yes. Electric razor? Sure. But a razor blade? There must be boundaries when a person attacks their nether regions, and I clearly have trouble with boundaries. I was a spur-of-the-moment girl. I sometimes forget to pause and think before acting.

"You cut your what?!?" my stunned fiancé asked.

I pointed to the area underneath my robe where I had a washcloth pressed to my crotch.

"I'd show you, but I'm trying to stop the bleeding. I thought mouths bled like a mother, but holy hell."

"Maybe a Band-Aid?"

My only response was to burst out laughing. I heard Dani come down the hallway and knock.

"Come in!" called Erik.

~

As soon as Dani stopped laughing, and the blood stopped seeping, I kicked Erik out of the room so we could start doing hair, Dani's first.

Once the curling iron heated, she sprayed a protectant and started separating her hair. In no time at all, her hair fell in long wavy tendrils. If my hair turned out half as beautiful, I'd be a happy bride. Dani's hair is thicker than mine, but our length is similar, almost hitting the waist.

"It looks amazing," I told her. "You are stunning from head to toe. Don't you know you're not supposed to upstage the bride on her wedding day?"

"Yours is going to look even better with the white streaks running through it." Dani searched my face. "And your makeup is perfect."

"Not too many wrinkles showing?"

"No. Not too many."

I stuck my tongue out at her. "I'm ready for my transformation."

Dani worked her magic, and I felt like a fairy princess in my colorful dress and long curls. She helped me pin a ring of dried flowers and herbs into my hair.

She clapped her hands together and pulled me up to stand in front of the full-length mirror.

"You look gorgeous. The most beautiful bride ever in history. Dad can't see you from this point on until the ceremony."

"He's going to need to get dressed."

"Show me his clothes. I'll put them in my room so he can change there. You stay here." She pointed to the chair. "Sit. Touch nothing, don't scratch any itches, don't pluck anything, don't pee."

"I can't pee?"

"Remember, pee has ammonia. That might sting a bit considering your… um…" Dani pointed at my crotch area. "… injury."

"Dammit."

As promised, Dani brought Erik's clothing to her room and told her dad he would not be allowed to look at me until the ceremony.

"How can I possibly wait that long to see her?" I heard him say outside the bedroom door.

"Dad. It's like 20 minutes."

"Guess I'd better shower soon."

"DAD!"

"I'll be done and downstairs in fifteen. You can bet on it."

"Why am I the only one stressing about pulling off this wedding on time and without injury? One thing already happened!"

"Did the bleeding finally stop?"

"Gosh, Dad. I assume so. I didn't look, and Sara didn't offer to show me. Go shower, please?"

Dani came in and reported that all of our guests were seated: Ethan and his family along with Lucas and Emily, Dad's sponsor, Daniel, Barb, and Rachel and Lisa, Tristan's moms. She was incredibly relieved that Tristan had opted not to come, avoiding that awkwardness for now at least.

She told me Lisa was in the guest bedroom practicing tying the ribbons for our handfast, since we'd chosen a pagan ceremony, and would head downstairs soon. Her dad was already out of the shower and in Dani's room, dressing.

The moment was almost here. From the first time I laid eyes on Erik that day in Lavallette, when I was digging holes in the sand so I could accommodate my boobs as I sunbathed, I knew he was my "one." Well, to be honest, I knew I wanted to sleep with him. I didn't know at that point that he was my "one."

But when he dropped to his knees in the middle of my flooded driveway just a couple of weeks later, he made my dreams come true, and he's been making them come true daily ever since.

I heard Erik whistling a cheery song in the hall and it faded as he walked downstairs. That meant it was almost time for me to descend the staircase and marry that handsome guy.

The doorbell rang. Who was at the door? Everyone was here. It was 11:55 a.m. and I should be walking down the stairs to my family and friends. We should be hearing Pachelbel's Canon in D, not a doorbell.

Commotion. Dani's voice, then Erik's.

Our bedroom was just far enough away to make the words inaudible. But I didn't like the tone from Dani and definitely not from Erik. My heart started beating a little faster, and I felt a little tickle in my intestines. Something felt off. Everything felt perfectly fine a little while ago when I cleansed and blessed the room. But now, something felt... off.

More voices. I was just about to open my bedroom door so I could hear what was going on when Erik and Dani walked in.

Their faces were almost comically scared. They were both terrified to tell me something. Except I already knew. I knew Cynthia would show up just when I was marrying her ex-husband.

"Sara..." Erik started but fell silent.

"Stop. You don't even have to tell me. Cynthia is here, isn't she? I knew it." I looked at Dani. "Didn't I say this would happen? She probably has a gun in her purse, too." My blissful mood was blown to shit, and I didn't even care that this had spoiled my big dress reveal.

Dani put her hands up as if to soothe me. "No, Sara, please don't be upset. She was trying to be here earlier, but traffic held them up and then there was an issue with their hotel, and she got here as soon as she could so she could see me." Dani hung her head. "It's all my fault."

"Erik? Can't she just leave and come back in a few hours?"

"Well, funny thing. It's more than that. I think you might want to come downstairs and see for yourself."

"But I'm in my wedding dress and ready to get married! I don't want to go schmooze Cynthia! I don't even want her here!"

I felt tears of frustration sting my eyes but refused to ruin my perfect makeup on Cynthia's behalf.

Do not give her that power. Easier said than done, I argued with my inner Goddess.

Call your power back, Sara.

I swear that was Lily's voice, not my inner Goddess. As if on cue, Kat pushed open the bedroom door and came to sit in front of me.

Call your power back.

Yes, ma'am.

I took a deep breath. "Let's go greet our new guests." My words sounded brave, but inside my guts were still considering letting me poop myself.

Erik looked even more alarmed now. "Sara, why are you so calm suddenly? You're not going to punch something, are you?" Erik was well aware of my temper. He had never seen it in action, but I'd told him stories. "You look beautiful, by the way." He smiled softly.

"Were you afraid I was going to punch you?" I laughed.

"Sometimes when you get calm like that, things happen."

"Nonsense. Let's greet everyone. Then we'll get married. If she wants to watch that, let her."

"Um, again, it's a bit more than that. Please, let's go downstairs." Erik's face was white.

My guts rolled.

"Hang on a second. I need to make sure I'm not going to poop."

I took some deep breaths, closed my eyes, and regained my

power. At least over my bowels. For the moment, anyway. The rest could still be a shitshow, figuratively speaking.

"Let's go."

I'm not sure what I was prepared for. What could be worse than Erik's ex-wife showing up at our wedding?

Halfway down the stairs I paused, my palm on the banister went clammy, and I imagine my face resembled a fish out of water, gasping for breath. I felt Erik's arms steady me from behind. Dani followed Erik, wringing her hands and making some mewling noises that sounded like she was saying *sorrysorrysorrysorrysorry*.

I was prepared for Cynthia. And her husband, Chris. I certainly wasn't prepared for the couple standing behind them.

"Sara! Surprise!" In a sickeningly sweet drawl with a side of snark, Drea called out her greeting.

Drea was standing at the bottom of the stairs. And not just Drea. Ron. My freaking ex-husband. First, I did not know they were still together. Second, what the hell were they doing here? On my wedding day? Cynthia looked like she had swallowed something distasteful, but she was always a little pinched, so it was hard to tell. Ron looked as if he was trying to melt into the wall behind him, like Homer Simpson backing up into the hedge. Chris stood with his hands clasped in front of him like he was about to pray, and I felt like they all should start praying I didn't lose my shit.

Lisa and Barb moved closer to the action; you don't mess with the Cell. Those two might not take a bullet for me, but they'd throw Drea out for me.

"You good, Sara?" Barb looked ready to rumble.

"I'm not sure, honestly. Stay close." I finished descending the stairs.

Dani was still making funny noises behind Erik. I turned around and looked at my almost-husband.

"What's happening? Why is my ex-husband here? What's going on?!?" I was panicking. "Erik? Do something."

"There's a very logical explanation," Cynthia said. "We met Drea and Ron on the cruise and became fast friends. We traveled together, so they joined us for our detour here to see Dani. I couldn't remember what time your wedding was, so I took a chance. I did not know you all knew each other until now."

Her left eye twitched, and Cynthia dropped her gaze. She was lying. Or she was having a reaction to too much Botox. Or both.

Chris looked at Cynthia in disbelief. "Darling, we knew. Why would you say that? We learned it the first week together."

Cynthia looked at the floor, not answering her husband.

Everyone's eyes were on Dani's mother. Including Dani's.

"Mom? Did you do this on purpose?"

"I thought it would be a funny surprise."

Erik reached my side in time to hold me back. I was ready to physically put them all out of my home.

Dani came up alongside me, clearly standing firmly on our side. "Mom, this is terrible. Why would you think bringing Sara's ex-husband to her wedding would be a fun surprise? And Drea too? It's bad enough *you're* crashing it." Dani burst out crying. "I'm so sorry, Sara."

I broke Erik's iron grip to get to Dani.

"Don't you dare cry. This is not your fault." I hugged her to me. "You're ruining your makeup. Go on up and fix yourself. I have a man to marry."

Dani sniffed back tears and nodded. "I'm so sorry."

"You're fine. I'm not mad. At least not at you. Your mother is another story."

I turned my attention back to the unwanted foursome near the front door. By now, all our guests had gathered in the foyer, and Barb and Lisa were inching closer to the offending wedding crashers.

I looked pointedly at my ex. "Ron, I'm surprised you went

along with this. You had to have known I wouldn't want any of you here on my wedding day."

"Cynthia was so sure everyone would laugh, so I didn't argue. I'm sorry, Sara."

"You've been around Drea too long. You're just as manipulative as she is."

"Excuse me?" The slow drawl was replaced with an indignant, shrill voice. "Don't call me manipulative. I see you're just as much of a bitch as you always were."

"I want all four of you out of this house right now," Erik growled. "You are not welcome here."

"You can't keep me away from my daughter, Erik. She's an adult."

"Get out, Mom." Dani appeared at the top of the stairs. "You shouldn't have done this. But now isn't the time to discuss it. Go away. I'll text you later."

Kat was standing next to Dani, her puff of white hair standing straight up, her tail twitching back and forth. From the bottom of the stairs, I could hear Kat's low growl.

"You both have this all wrong. I just wanted to see Dani for the holiday."

"Cynthia!" Chris's voice was stern. "Let's go. We have a lot to talk about."

"Dani?" Cynthia refused to give up.

"Mom. Just go. Please."

Erik moved from behind me and crossed the last bit of floor between him and the two couples.

"Erik, it's so nice to see you," Drea purred, sticking her double Ds out as far as they could reach.

Nice to see some things never changed.

"Get out, Drea." Erik pushed past the four interlopers and held open the front door. "Now."

"Erik, I really think you're overreacting here," Cynthia said.

"Out. All of you. Go back to the cave you crawled out of. Stay there. Do not come back here. If you want to see Dani, you'll have to see her somewhere else."

"Fine. Text me later, Dani. Please." Cynthia moved towards the doorway. "I'm sorry, Sara, for what that's worth. I obviously made a poor decision."

"Good day, Cynthia. Now leave." I looked around the room. "Would someone please hand me the broom from the kitchen?"

Ethan obliged, back with it in a wink, and as the four least-welcome people exited my home, I swept behind them. More than once. Then I turned the broom upside down and tapped the handle on the ground three times.

When I turned around, all eyes were on me.

"Just cleaning up." I smiled. "Can I please get married now?"

"What was that you did with the broom?" Erik whispered.

"Just a stop visiting spell. Nothing too serious."

"You aren't going to hurt Cynthia, are you?"

"Me? Never. Black magic is not my way." I paused. "But it is tempting. I will not lie about that."

"How about Drea?"

"Also tempting. But I don't need that kind of energy coming back at me."

There was an incident involving diarrhea that proved the dark arts were something I should not explore. Let's just leave it at that.

Erik moved everyone back into their seats in the living room. I made my way upstairs and checked my face quickly in the bathroom. Other than bitchy, I looked just like I did when this started. Makeup still flawless, hair still wavy, dress perfect. I made silly faces at myself in the mirror until the bitchy look was gone. Time to get this done. No interruptions this time. No unpleasant surprises. Just my "one," my family, and my friends. At the last moment, I shoved my pink vibrator-looking fan into the pocket of the layered dress. It was small enough nobody would notice.

I heard Pachelbel's Canon start up, and I made my way to the top of the stairs. Gripping the handrail, I slowly made my way down, so I didn't make the trip on my ass. This time, I put everything out of my head except Erik. With each step, I thought of another reason I loved him so much.

He treats me like a queen.

He laughs at my terrible jokes.

He cooks.

He gives amazing foot rubs.

He's a good kisser. Among other things.

He supports whatever ideas I come up with, no matter how strange.

He's kind and generous.

At this point, my brain stopped coordinating my list with my feet, and I almost lost my balance. So, I concentrated on getting down the steep stairs and nothing else. By the time I had hit bottom, I was cursing my idea of coming down the stairs. I should have just come in from the kitchen. Much less stressful.

Lisa was standing near the Christmas tree, Erik beside her, holding the ribbons we would use for the handfasting.

I stepped into the living room with a smile on my face and lots of love in my heart. But then the whole Cynthia and Drea thing bubbled up. I wished all of them everything they deserved. I had hoped to never lay eyes on Drea again. Even Ron and I had no connection with each other anymore, thanks to the fact that we never had children. So, to see them both, together, in my living room, on today of all days, was still gnawing at my gut. Was this awful woman going to haunt my life forever?

My face must have clouded over with that thought as I approached the front of the room, because Erik leaned over to me and asked if I was okay.

"I'm fine. Honest." Imagining a little whisk broom sweeping them all out of my mind, I turned to Lisa and nodded, and Pachelbel stopped.

Lisa took the ribbons from Erik and gently tied them around one of our wrists, so we were bound. As she wrapped, Lisa told the story of handfasting and what it meant. She spoke of the symbolic ritual of binding a couple's hands together, literally tying the knot. The ribbons and knots represent their commitment and unity.

Just as my dear friend tied the last knot, I felt a hot flash creep up. I could feel my face turning red. Why now? At this moment, when I only had one working hand, and I was the center of attention at my wedding ceremony?

Of course, my little fan was in my right pocket, and my right hand was currently attached to Erik's left. I reached across my body with my left hand and tried to gain access to the pocket, but I failed miserably. I could only imagine what this looked like from behind.

"What's the matter?" Erik whispered.

"Hot flash. I need my fan."

"Your hand is soaking wet."

"I'm aware. Help me get my fan out."

By now my face was wet, and a drip fell into my eye, stinging and probably ruining my perfect makeup. Lisa magically pulled a tissue out of thin air and handed it to me, nodding knowingly.

I turned to face our guests. "I swear we're not jinxed; it's just a hot flash. Please stand by."

Erik finally found my pocket with his right hand and pulled out the pink vibrator-shaped fan. Every single woman in the living room laughed. Until I opened it and hit the power button. Then they all turned jealous. I could tell.

"Only you." Erik shook his head and stuck another of Lisa's tissues into our clasped hands to sop up the drippage. "Thank you for making me laugh every day since I met you."

I directed the fan with my left hand and the breeze on my face was nirvana. I was ever so grateful the dress was multicolored and wouldn't show any dampness.

"Please pull my neckline out so I can fan my tatas?"

Lisa snorted and Erik gladly obliged, peeking down the front of my dress until I bopped him on the head with the fan.

"Should we take a break so you can cool off? I can undo the ribbons," Lisa offered.

"I just need to step outside in the cold air for two minutes. Erik, you'll have to come with me. I don't want to wait to be untied."

"There's nowhere else I'd rather be but tied to you."

"Forgive me, everyone," I announced grandly. "Chat amongst yourselves. We'll be right back."

"Can I get a coat or something?" Erik asked. "It's freezing out there!"

"No time! No time!"

"I'll throw you one," Lucas said, and grabbed his coat off the pile in the dining room.

Erik caught the flying coat with his outstretched right hand and did his best to drape it around his shoulders. "Thanks, buddy."

I exited the front door with Erik on my heels. Not that he had any choice.

We hit the front porch and the frigid air, and I immediately felt better. I kept the fan going and dabbed my face with the ribbons until Erik pulled our hands away.

"Is it good luck to sweat all over our handfasting?"

"Beats the crap out of me. I had to stop the sweat drops from hitting my eyes because those hurt. The ribbons need to understand."

Erik kissed the top of my head. "Your hair is a little damp."

"I'm a mess." I laughed. "This simple wedding has turned into a circus."

"I would expect nothing less from you, my love."

"Can we please get married now? I think I'm done. I could use another tissue, though. The one between our hands is soaked."

Erik pulled a clean tissue from his pocket. "I thought there might be crying."

"Still time."

"True. You haven't heard my vows yet."

I dabbed the tissue against my face with my free left hand. Unfortunately, I am not ambidextrous, and Erik watched my clumsy attempts with a grin.

"Let me." He took the tissue from my hand and lightly patted my face, cleaning the mascara debris left by the offending sweat drops. "I haven't told you some good news."

"I need some good news right now. Spill it."

"I was talking to Rachel, and she offered to stay at our house for the two weeks we're away. There are a few flea markets in the area she wants to check out. The dogs love her already, and I'm sure Kat will adjust."

"That is good news! A big worry off my shoulders. Lisa doesn't mind her being away for that long?"

"She said it was fine and would come visit on her days off from the store."

This was awesome news. The last stumbling block before our trip. Now I could relax and plan for our time away without that huge worry. The animals would be in great hands, and our home wouldn't be empty.

Finally feeling chilled, I slipped the vibrator fan into my pocket —my left one this time—just in case another hot flash hit and I needed it quickly.

"Let's go get married," I declared.

CHAPTER 49

DANI

As I watched Sara lead my dad outside, I felt like a piece of crap. This was all my fault. I should have known my mother would do something like that. I understood perfectly why she and Drea would have become friends, and I knew they had planned their arrival time on purpose. Drea would do anything to get back at Sara. Even after all this time, and even though Drea had Ron, she was still jealous of Sara.

"Why are you so sad, Dani?" Jace looked worried.

"I feel like this whole thing is my fault."

"You made her have a hot flash?"

"No. But the stress probably helped bring it on. So maybe, yeah, the hot flash is my fault too."

Rachel, overhearing us, leaned in. "Dani, this is not your fault. You can't control what other people choose to do."

"You sound like Sara."

"I'll take that as a compliment. Sara can be wise. So can your dad. You know damn well Sara won't blame you for any of this."

I knew that, but it only helped take away a little of the sadness.

This wasn't the wedding Sara had been planning for. It would be memorable, but not for the right reasons.

This is not your fault.

Sara's voice came through my mind loud and clear. I still got startled when this happened, but I no longer questioned it.

My dad entered the front door first with Sara close behind, not that the ribbons tying them together would let them be any farther apart. Before they walked back to stand in front of Lisa one more time, she pulled him towards my chair.

"This is not your fault. Do you hear me?"

"I heard you say it a moment ago, too."

"Oh good. It's working." Sara tapped her temple. "I was afraid it was off-line."

"No. You came through loud and clear. I'm trying not to be sad, but right now you need to forget about me and get married so we can start the party!"

Sara nodded in agreement, and they turned around to face Lisa.

Lisa grinned. "It's time for the vows you wrote to each other. Are you ready?"

"Abso-freaking-lutely." Sara pulled her notes from her left pocket, and her vibrator fan crashed to the floor, the plastic case breaking. "Dammit. This is not good. I swear we're jinxed."

Kat appeared out of nowhere and batted the fan out of the way, then sat down next to where Sara stood and looked up at her. Not to be outdone, Molly moved from her spot and sat next to Kat. Of course, whatever Molly does, Tank must try, so he climbed out of his dog bed, stretched, farted loudly, and moved into position next to Molly. It was the most amazing and magical bridal party in history.

The air was still ripe as my dad and Sara started their vows, and more than a few of us held tissues to our noses for reasons other than emotion.

Jace grabbed my hand and squeezed it. His touch gave me butterflies, which filled my entire body, and the back of my head erupted in chills that started at the back of my neck. Head chills mean the right path, at least according to Sara. Kat took her eyes off Sara and looked straight into mine. One slow blink, then she returned her attention to Sara.

Piece by piece, my life seemed to be jelling into something quite exciting.

CHAPTER 50

SARA

"Sara, the moment I saw you digging in the sand is forever etched in my brain. That night I watched you dance on the porch made me yearn for you in a way I've never felt."

Dammit, I knew he could see me that night.

"Watching you fall in love with my daughter, us developing a strong relationship, and then being lucky enough to be the recipient of your love... It's simply magic. You make my days and nights bliss, even when you snore."

I laughed and poked him in the stomach.

"I promise to love you and cherish you until my last breath. Thank you for making my life so beautiful. I am forever yours."

My voice caught in my throat, and I was afraid I was going to cry. I swallowed a hiccup and looked down at my notes.

"Erik, your—"

The sound of a tractor trailer interrupted me as it passed the house heading towards the bridge, a police car, lights flashing, right behind him. I knew what was coming next. Traffic would back up, and the horn honking would begin as they tried to turn the enormous truck around. The traffic was heavier because of the holiday, and it was a popular no-toll bridge so it wouldn't be long before the cacophony of horns and back-up beeps would steal my vow time. Do I wait it out? Talk fast?

I talked fast. Erik knew exactly what was happening and waited expectantly.

"Erik, my life has been nothing but blessed in our time together. You make my days bright and my nights safe and warm."

The first honk.

"Thank you for supporting all my ideas, no matter how silly they sound. Thank you for being my partner in every sense of the word."

Honk. Honk. Back-up beeps. Dammit. I peeked over Lisa's shoulder and out the window. Cars were already lining up past our home, and tempers were likely short. I wondered how many hang-overs were sitting out there.

"Just finish it," I whispered to Lisa. "This is about to get even louder."

"What?"

"Just finish, it's loud."

"I'm just going to finish, okay? It's getting loud."

My life is a circus. I nodded gratefully.

"By the power vested in me, I now pronounce you husband and wife. You may kiss the bride!"

Cheers erupted from behind us as Erik softly kissed my lips. It was official. I had married the man I'd waited my entire life for.

Dani joined us in a group hug. "Congratulations, Daddy! Congratulations, Step-Mommy!"

"Evil Step-Mommy, and don't you forget it." I grinned through my tears.

The rest of the guests huddled around us, handing out hugs and kisses and well wishes. Lisa untied our hands, and the soggy tissue dropped to the floor, quickly batted out of the way by Kat.

The truck finally got turned around, and traffic once again flowed past our house, peace restored.

Sun broke through the clouds and streamed through the windows, throwing rainbow prisms on the walls and floor from the crystals I had strung.

I looked around the room at our guests celebrating our union, and a feeling of great peace came over me. I felt Kat rub against my leg and bent to pick her up.

"I know in my heart that you're Lily," I told her.

One slow blink.

"And I think you have much to teach me, don't you?"

Another slow blink and her paw reached up to touch my face.

"Sara! Come join us!" Diana called from the dining room, where the delicious Thai food had just been delivered.

Kat jumped down from my arms and ran to the room with the food. Molly and Tank were already at their stations, ready for handouts.

I never ask the Universe "what else can happen" because the Universe has a sense of humor and she will answer that question. Instead, I sent a blessing to her and thanked her for letting us get through the ceremony (mostly) intact.

I felt my husband come up from behind and wrap his arms around me.

"Come join us, Mrs. Hanson. The food is hot and the #25 is awaiting my wife."

"My favorite," I murmured. "Now, how are we going to get rid of all these guests so we can make mad, passionate wedding love?"

Dani laughed. "Can't you give it a rest for one afternoon, please?"

"Don't speak to your step-mommy like that." Erik chuckled.

"I'm talking to both of you! I'm handing out earplugs to Barb and Lisa. They don't deserve to hear what's going to happen tonight."

"Keep a pair for yourself, kiddo."

"Oh, don't you worry, earplugs and noise-canceling headphones are my friend."

"Don't forget your emotional support nuts."

"Yes, and my nuts."

"Wait, what?" Jace's face was priceless. "You have emotional support nuts? What does that mean?"

"I'll explain it after we eat." Dani pulled Jace by the arm. "C'mon. I'm starving."

Jace looked back at me. "Emotional support nuts?"

"Welcome to the family, Jace."

Later that night, when the guests were long gone and everyone staying at our place was tucked into their beds, my husband and I held each other tightly.

"I think things are heating up between Dani and Jace." I trailed my finger along his shoulder. "He seems like a good kid. Her life may take an interesting turn."

"As long as she doesn't move to Australia."

"Well, thanks. I hadn't thought of that possibility."

"Could happen. I guess we'll just have to wait and see." He pulled away and kissed me. "Happy New Year, Mrs. Hanson."

"Happy New Year, Mr. Hanson."

The moonlight broke through the clouds and lit his handsome face, looking at me with so much love in his eyes. "How did I get so lucky?" he asked.

"Luck has nothing to do with it, my love. I manifested you."

"So, I had no choice but to fall in love with you?"

"That's correct. Are you mad?"

"Far from it," Erik said. "Thank you for seeing me."

"You're welcome. And ditto."

"How could I help but see you, Sara? You're what makes my world colorful in all the ways."

Erik nuzzled his face into my neck, deeply breathing my scent, his body relaxing as if I were a sedative. We fell asleep in each other's arms, our foreheads pressed together, perhaps to join in our dreams as well.

Kat gave a nod to something no one else could see and purred, continuing her grooming with a slow blink.

The End

ACKNOWLEDGMENTS

You know that old saying, it takes a village? That works for writing a book, too. In no particular order, because each person was integral in getting *Charms & Chapters* published.

My husband Jeff, for his unwavering support and unconditional love.

My Cell.

My Dawgs.

Jeffrey Metzger for my author and cover photos, going above and beyond, thank you.

Barb LeMasters for knowing where to send me for editing.

Kim & Lucas Mason for opening your home to me. Sara & family needed a place to live and you provided that beautifully. I'm sorry if It's weird that I lived in your house with you, albeit virtually, for 8 months.

Diana Pickford for all the tarot help. I know just enough to be dangerous, so I called in an expert.

Thai at the Palace and Infloressense for giving me the needed visual for the bookstore and gallery.

Charlie Ohlweiler for the cover art idea. I never would have thought of it until your comment "Cover art?"

Barbie Halaby with Monocle Editing for amazing editing, it gives me chills. *wink*

Norman Worth and Bert Baron from WRNJ radio in Hackettstown NJ for giving me airtime to promote my books and not 'forgetting to turn my mic on' like my husband sometimes does during our show on WNTI.

ABOUT THE AUTHOR

Charms and Chapters is author Alexandra Rusch's second novel. "Sandi" lives in gorgeous Warren County NJ with her husband Jeff, and various fur-faces. She is an artist, potter, and a Jersey Girl, born and bred.

If you enjoyed *Charms and Chapters*, please consider leaving a review on Amazon, Goodreads, or your favorite review site. Thank you!